There are vampires wailing rattling and people screaming glide over our heads and the a mixture of hot dogs, chips, sauce.

'What shall we shoot first,' asks Mr Hoyland.

'Well, we could start with Sister Frances,' Marie giggles.

'We'd better do the parts where we're in costume first,' she says out loud. 'Then people can take their clothes and props back to the bus.'

Marie opens her brochure to the map on the first page. 'We need to find Dracula's Castle,' she explains.

We start to thread our way through the park. Near the gate are rows of stalls selling food and souvenirs. There are black rubber bats dangling on elastic, plastic masks and totem poles. Other stalls sell badges, stickers, mugs and T-shirts saying, *Nightmare Park – A Journey into Fear* and *I Rode the Nightmare* and Survived.

NIGHTMARE PARK

LINDA HOY

An Armada original

This book is dedicated to all the school pupils who have inspired me with their enthusiasm and creativity whilst inventing and writing their own Nightmare Parks.

Nightmare Park was first published in the U.K. in Armada in 1988

Armada is an imprint of the Children's Division, part of the Collins Publishing Group, 8 Grafton Street, London W1X 3LA

© 1988 Linda Hoy

Printed and bound in Great Britain by William Collins Sons & Co. Ltd., Glasgow

ROBBO'S STORY

'Shall we go on the ghost train, then?'

That was Robbo and he's a friend of mine. Well, when I say *friend*, what I mean is that we go around together. Actually, we're very different. My name's Jim and I'm small and fairly quiet and a bit on the weedy side and Robbo's big and loud-mouthed with huge shoulders and a square head that makes him look like the front end of a juggernaut. We've been going around together all today – Robbo and me and some of the others from down at the club. Today was our annual outing to Blackpool, you see – a day out at the seaside. We come here every year.

We set off early this morning and got here round about lunchtime. Since then we've been having a right laugh. We walked down onto the beach, skimming screwed-up chip papers and dead fish into the water and then, all of a sudden, Robbo ran up behind young Jonathan, lifted him onto his shoulders and ran off with him right out to sea. We all stood laughing as Robbo chucked Jonathan into the water and then we watched him staggering out dripping with bits of seaweed and strips of sodden bog roll on his head.

We always laugh at Jonathan. His mum and dad are really posh. They come down the club to fetch him in their car so he never has to walk home on his own.

Anyway, after all of us had had a paddle, we sent Jonathan to have his fortune told. Robbo shoved him in, still dripping, through the caravan door marked *Petronella, Princess of the Paranormal* whilst Robbo himself pranced around the caravan shouting, 'Oyay, the secret life of

Jonathan Staveley. All is being revealed!' He kept rattling on the door as well. Until Petronella, rushed out and swore at him and clipped him round the earhole.

'What did she tell you then?' we asked Jonathan when he came out.

He was looking really smug. 'She said I'm going to be a great musician,' he told us, beaming all over his face. We all fell about with laughing then because Jonathan's completely tone deaf and he has about as much sense of rhythm as a plate of Blackpool whelks. Boiled ones. You should see him trying to dance. He swings his great long gangling arms from side to side like an elastic gorilla and sticks his feet out at right angles like a frog. Robbo's always trying to make Jonathan get up and dance. He tells him how he's really good. He only says it so everybody else can have a laugh.

They persuaded me to have my fortune told next. I can't really say I was impressed. Princess Petronella told me that I was going to have a long journey very soon but, of course, everybody has a long journey home from Blackpool, don't they? She also said that, before I went home today, I was going to get a nasty shock. I didn't take much notice of that because you have one shock after another when you're out with Robbo. Especially when he's wearing his King Kong mask.

*

They'd done the ghost train up really well. It was like a big, old-fashioned castle with an enormous skeleton leaning across the roof. They'd fixed the skeleton so that its jaws kept opening and closing. It was very clever, that. In the middle of the castle, where you climbed into the little cars, they had a vampire bat flying round and a black witch whizzing past on a broomstick with a cat behind her. After the cars had gone into the ghost train, there were these

6

towers at the side where they came into the open again and went back through black rubber doors with a portcullis painted on them. They have doors like that in hospitals for the stretchers to go through but they don't have paintings on.

Robbo and I went on together. I felt shown up at first because he would insist on wearing this King Kong mask that he'd bought from a joke shop down the other end of the Golden Mile. It looked revolting. It was made of that soft, green, crinkly plastic and had horrible bulging eyeballs with slits in the middle to see out of. It made him look really obnoxious and people kept standing open-mouthed and gawping at him. But, apart from having to sit next to Robbo wearing that revolting mask, the ghost train was really great.

You went into a long dark tunnel first, with pictures painted on the walls and they were shining – I think it's ultra-violet light that makes them glow like that in the dark. Anyway, it was all spooky with cobwebs dangling down and brushing past your face like daddy-long-legs drifting on you in the dark.

I thought it was good, but Robbo kept saying things like: 'This is rubbish' and, 'Anybody can see it's all plastic.' You know, stuff like that.

There was a skull hanging from the roof of the tunnel and then, later on, this head. Just when you were riding up to it, it sort of toppled over and its eyeballs fell out of their sockets. I suppose they were on pieces of invisible thread or something because they didn't actually fall down into the carriage with you – they just sort of hung there, on this face. I started wishing I hadn't just eaten two cartons of curry sauce, a bag of chips, a candy floss, two hot dogs, a plate of prawns and a choc-ice because they all started churning round together in my stomach.

After a bit, the carriage came into the open and you got a

look at the fair and all the people queuing up for rides and then you juddered round the corner and through the swing doors, back inside. There were all sorts of different ghosts and skeletons and things. There was a coffin where the lid opened by itself when you went past. Robbo was still making out that he wasn't impressed although he'd been quite taken with the head with the eyeballs or, perhaps I should say, without the eyeballs.

There was one other really grisly thing we went past and that was a coffin standing upright with its lid half-open. On the inside of the lid were long rusty bloodstained nails sticking out and, inside the coffin, the body of a woman. I suppose it must have been made of wax or something. Her body had all these gaping red wounds from where the nails were supposed to have stuck in and I felt the curry and the choc-ice rising into my throat again. 'Look at that,' said Robbo, leaning across and pointing. 'A 'uman dartboard!' That's his idea of humour.

Anyway, the ghost train came into the open again with a big dipper thing in the middle, except that the dip didn't really go down very far – not like it does on a proper roller coaster – then, back inside, just before the end was this really clever part – like an avalanche. What happened was that the walls of the ghost train were lit up and painted with stone and pebbles and they rotated – you know, like they kept turning over and over. It made you feel as if it was you that was falling about. It made you feel really dizzy.

''ey up!' said Robbo. 'Have we been boozin' or what?' He was trying to laugh about it but, from the way he was clinging hold of the skeleton's arm that they had for a handrail, I could tell he wasn't too keen.

*

'What's it like, then?' Jonathan asked us. He was standing outside the *Magnolia Café* with a big box of popcorn in his hand.

I opened my mouth to tell him it was great but I looked at Robbo first.

'It wa' rubbish,' Robbo sneered. 'It were just for little kids. Weren't it?' he asked me.

'Yeah,' I said.

He'd taken his mask off now. I was very pleased because one little old granny had nearly had a nervous breakdown when he'd jumped out in front of her while she was waiting for the Alice in Wonderland train. In fact the White Rabbit had to sit her down on a plastic toadstool and give her two glasses of brandy before she was fit to move off. It's not safe to walk around in things like that.

*

We were standing around then with nothing much to do and I could see that Robbo was thinking. You notice that because, for Robbo, it's very unusual. He's more what you'd call a lad of action – you know, he acts first and thinks afterwards or, more likely, he never thinks at all.

All of a sudden, he started grinning. 'Hey, I've got an idea, Jim,' he said. He glanced around at Jonathan who was still up to his nose in popcorn. 'Do you think we can get Johnny to go on the ghost train?'

'I don't know.'

'We could scare him.' Robbo lowered his voice and put his head down next to mine – it's not a pretty sight either – all spots and blackheads. 'Look, we could go on the ghost train again and get out. We could wait for him coming and then jump out on him . . . we could . . .'

'Don't be daft,' I told him.

'What's daft about it, hey? He'd be terrified. We could

9

sneak up behind him and pretend to strangle him. We could . . .'

What did he think we were? Leaping about in a ghost train like a pair of plastic poltergeists . . . 'Don't be stupid,' I told him.

'Stupid? It'll be a right laugh. He'll be terrified. They'll be able to hear him screamin' from the top of t' Blackpool Tower.'

That's an exaggeration. The Tower's right at the other end of the Golden Mile.

'Look, I'll tell you what . . .' Robbo was getting really worked up about it now, his face bulging red with excitement like an overripe tomato, '. . . one of us could climb in next to him in the dark and grab him by the neck. It'd be a right laugh.'

'How would we get out of the ghost train?' I asked him. 'We can't just open those doors in front of everybody and walk out.'

Robbo thought for a minute. 'If I climb in next to Johnny,' he explained, 'you could climb in next to somebody else – the next car that comes past with only one person in it. Pull your coat down over your head and they'd think you were a ghost. They'd think it was part of the ride.'

'Don't be stupid.'

I could just imagine myself clambering in next to some old biddy and getting belted over the head with her umbrella. Or crouching behind a coffin trying to impersonate Dracula every time a carriage full of people came past. 'I think it'd only work if you did it on your own,' I told him. 'Two of us would just get in each other's way.'

'Do you reckon?'

I shouted across to Jonathan before Robbo had time to think it out. 'Fetch us some popcorn, Johnny,' I yelled.

'Get your own.'

'Go on. I'll pay for you to go on the ghost train if you do.'

Jonathan walked towards the popcorn stall.

'Are you going to do it, then?' I said to Robbo.

'Course I am,' Robbo chuckled. 'I'll wait near the end – by that avalanche. It was good, that bit.'

I didn't say anything about how he made out the ghost train was rubbish before. That was how he always was – acting tough. He was dead soft really.

Then Robbo frowned a bit. 'I say, he will come up behind me, won't he? I mean, them carriages can't overtake each other, can they? Not like proper cars.'

Robbo had about as much skill in comprehension as a stick of Blackpool rock. 'No,' I told him, as if I was explaining it to a six-year-old. 'No, they can't overtake each other. Not like proper cars.'

'You just watch out for him when he comes out through the doors on that tower. He'll be screamin' his pants off.' Robbo did an impersonation of Jonathan rolling his eyeballs round and shaking like a custard with convulsions. Both of us laughed although it did occur to me that there was quite a strong chance of Jonathan having a heart attack. I remembered the time he had to go on tranquillisers after he found the dead rat that Robbo had hidden in his school sandwich box, but I decided there was no use worrying about that.

Jonathan came back then with a big bag of popcorn for me. 'Here you are,' he said. 'Are you paying for me to go on the ghost train, then?'

'I'll think about it,' I told him. 'You don't mind going on your own, do you?'

*

We got to the front of the queue and Robbo was getting more and more excited. He kept hopping from one foot to the other as if he was going to wet himself.

11

'Listen to that,' said Jonathan.

We could hear people screaming inside the ghost train. 'It'll be louder than that when you're inside, won't it, Johnny?' said Robbo, giving me a nudge.

Jonathan raised his eyebrows in disgust but just then an empty car trundled round the corner and Robbo jumped inside. It was number thirteen.

The next car arrived and Jonathan climbed in just as Robbo was disappearing through the black swing doors. 'I'll watch out for you,' I shouted. I pointed to where the cars came out of the doorway on the nearest black turret but Jonathan had already disappeared inside the tunnel.

As soon as they'd gone, I stepped back from the crowd so I could get a view of them both when they came out. A lot of cars came by with mums and dads and little kids in and then the car appeared that Robbo had gone in – number thirteen – and it was empty.

I couldn't understand that because Robbo wasn't supposed to be getting out until the avalanche and that was near the end.

'Hey up, Jim!'

The doors had opened again and Jonathan was trundling round the corner in his car, grinning and waving down at me like a kiddy having a donkey ride. I couldn't understand it. Why was he looking so cheerful? Why hadn't Robbo scared him stupid by now? And where was Robbo?

Jonathan turned and juddered back through the next set of doors and, as I waited for the cars to come down the dipper thing in the middle, I kept thinking to myself: surely the cars can't overtake each other like Robbo said? They can't have changed the numbers round. You think all sorts of stupid things when you can't understand what's going on. I wasn't scared or worried or anything. Not just then. Only puzzled.

After a few minutes, the empty car rolled down the dip.

12

Number thirteen. That's right. It was Robbo's car. There was something lying on the seat but I couldn't make out what it was. Something crumpled up. Then behind came Jonathan. He didn't look at all scared yet. When he saw me watching him, he grinned and waved again and then he grasped his hands around his throat as if somebody was throttling him. He was still laughing, though. Just having a joke.

I looked out for Robbo in all the other cars then. It was ridiculous; they were all full up. I thought I might have seen him staggering out through the black rubber doors on one of the towers, but I didn't. There was no sign of him anywhere.

*

Jonathan's car stopped in front of the cash desk and he climbed out and walked across. 'Hey, it was fantastic,' he told me. 'Did you see that woman in that coffin? With all those nails? Ugh!' He pulled a face. 'And that avalanche . . ?'

'Have you seen Robbo?' I interrupted him.

'Robbo? No.' Jonathan looked surprised. 'He went in before me, though, didn't he? He should be out by now.'

I had to explain to him then about how Robbo was hoping to jump off the ghost train and scare him. I felt a bit rotten about it but I put all the blame on Robbo. Of course it's easy to do that to somebody when they've disappeared. Then we walked over to the ghost train and started looking round.

We looked around for three hours. I went back to the coach park twice and, when Robbo wasn't there, I left a message on the windscreen of our coach telling him where to meet us when he got back. But he never did. I started getting worried. What made it worse was that all the others just treated it like a joke.

13

'He'll have jumped out on some bird in that ghost train,' one of them said. 'He'll still be riding round with her.' They all laughed.

'Yeah, they'll be having it off behind one of them plastic coffins.'

'Somebody'll have a shock when they come past.'

'Especially if he's still wearing his King Kong mask.'

Everybody laughed again. I didn't laugh, though. That King Kong mask. I remembered it then.

So I did what I should have done before and I went back to the woman on the cash desk at the ghost train. 'I've lost my friend,' I told her. 'You've not seen anybody hangin' about, have you?' I wished then I'd not put it like that because there was this vampire bat hanging from the ceiling and that witch on her broomstick as well.

The woman just shook her head.

'He was wearing a King Kong mask,' I told her. 'You've not seen one of those, have you?'

She reached underneath the drawer of the till and pulled out this crumpled mask. 'Is this it?' she asked me. 'We found it in one of the cars.'

I recognized it straightaway and reached to pick it up. Actually, I hate touching that thin, crinkly, rubbery stuff but I lifted it up anyway and smoothed out some of the creases. And then I realized something horrible. My stomach turned over and I felt all cold and shivery. This King Kong mask was supposed to have great big bulging eyeballs – it was the thing I hated most about it – and now somebody had cut the eyeballs out. Or ripped them out. They were sort of hanging off on threads. They looked horrible. I suppose Robbo must have done it for a laugh, but it didn't look funny somehow.

The other thing was that this mask was sort of stained around the bottom. A big mark all dried-up. Like blood. I shuddered and screwed the mask up and put it in my trouser pocket.

I went for a walk round then whilst I decided what to do. Just near the ghost train there's this glass cube with a jester or a clown or something in it. Laughing. I don't know if people have to put money in it or what. But you can hear it laughing all the time when you're walking past: *Ha ha ha haaaa. Ha ha ha haaaa*. I hate that noise. You'd never believe that the sound of somebody laughing could give you the creeps like that.

So then I did what I knew all the time I'd have to do. The thing I'd been dreading ever since I found that mask: I had to go back on the ghost train.

There was still a big queue and every minute that I waited seemed like half an hour because I was dreading getting near the front. I kept telling myself that it was only a fairground ride and there was nothing to worry about and Robbo would be all right really. But all the time I was terrified.

When it came to my turn to pay, I could hardly give the man my money – my hands were so sticky with sweat. I looked up and saw the big skeleton on top of the ghost train, gazing down at me and opening and closing its jaws. I swallowed hard and went and stood by the side of the track waiting for an empty carriage.

Whilst I was waiting, I noticed all the things that I hadn't noticed last time when it had all been just a joke. I saw how old everything looked – how black and gloomy. And then there was this musty, damp sort of a smell like you get in really old houses. It didn't seem all plastic and artificial any more. It seemed more . . . more sort of real.

And then the empty car came. The number, of course, was just a coincidence and you can't ask to get in a different carriage just because you don't like the number, can you? But there it was, anyway. I climbed into the car and I thought to myself; well, this is it. I didn't know what I was thinking I might do – shout out Robbo's name? Climb out and look for him? I don't know. I just thought that I was going to find out what happened to him somehow or other. And, of course, I did.

Well, that's not quite true. We never did find out what happened to Robbo. Ever. We didn't find out and the police didn't find out and, as far as I can see, nobody else did. I don't think they ever will. All I found out for certain on that ghost train ride was that, wherever Robbo'd got to, he was never coming back.

Anyway, this black car that I was in set off down the track towards the black swing doors and I suddenly had a feeling that I'd seen those doors somewhere else before – apart from in a hospital. In a crematorium. You know how, at a cremation service, they have the coffin on these sort of runners, and when it's time for it to get burnt up, the vicar presses a button somewhere and it all starts moving forward. It moves forwards through these curtains and behind them are these black rubber doors that swing open just like the ones that I was going through on the ghost train.

I looked all about me when I got inside and I thought about shouting out for Robbo but I didn't. I didn't need to.

I couldn't really explain to anybody what happened afterwards and, when I tried, they just told me I was hysterical. They said it was the worry and the upset that had made my mind go funny – you know, like seeing things.

But I know what I saw. I saw it so clearly that when I wake up in the middle of the night, sweating, I can still see everything exactly how it happened that day.

First there was the skeleton: the skull. Hanging down. Then there were all the other different ghosts and spooks painted on the walls. And then, coming up around the corner, that head that I told you about before. The one with the eyeballs.

The head was suspended on its own, high above the carriage and the eyeballs were protruding – kind of hanging

16

on stalks. As the carriage went past, the head sort of juddered. It seemed to be leering at me. And then the eyeballs fell, sort of trickling down the cheeks. And as they fell, and as I looked up at the face, I felt as if I knew exactly what had happened. My heart seemed to turn itself right over and I felt the blood drain from my face. There was no mistake about it: it was Robbo.

So, of course, nobody believes me. The detective said he got the face down later and it was nothing but a mask, a plastic fibreglass sort of model and, anyway, how could it be a human head? But I've never just imagined things before. I know exactly what I saw that day and, to the end of my life, I shall never forget it.

And, of course, they never explained the other thing. When I got to the end of the ghost train ride where all the cars set off from and where all the people queue up, there was this gravestone. Not a real gravestone, mind you; just a painting of one. But when I saw what was written on it, I felt all cold and shivery again. I gripped hold of the skeleton that they had for a handle at the side of the car and I nearly passed out with shock. It said:

HERE LIES

ROBBO

EX-GHOST TRAIN RIDER

HAPPY HAUNTING
JIM

And, if you don't believe it, just go to Blackpool sometime and go on that ghost train in the amusement park. You'll see what I mean.

WAYNE'S STORY

A JOURNEY

INTO *FEAR*

Nightmare Park!!
Tuesday

Dear Vi,

Well, here I am with a proper job at last. It's funny how I never thought I'd find any kind of a job, let alone anything as interesting as this. And, you know, I've always wanted to come to Nightmare Park. *Watching the ads on the telly –* Satan's Staircase *and the* Iron Maiden, Dracula's Castle *and the* Gingerbread House. *I used to think about both of us coming down here for the day. I used to think about us having a picnic together, then going on all the rides but, well . . . I could never afford it, could I? Things are changing though now – with a few more months on these wages – everything's starting to look up.*

I've been working on Dracula's Castle. *Painting it up. It looks exactly like it does on the posters: dark and bleak right at the top of a hill. Inside it's really spooky although I haven't explored it all yet. The whole place bristles with vampire bats, coffins with lids that open by themselves and strange ghosts that are really holograms – they look so realistic it's hard to believe there's not someone there in the room watching you. It's really eerie. I still feel scared about working inside on my own, even though I've been in there a dozen times now. It's not* so bad when there's a group of us – we have the radio on then or some tapes and we sit down for our lunch break in amongst the monsters with our sandwiches and mugs of tea.

It's just when I'm in there by myself . . . that's when I feel a bit funny. When I first went in the castle, I made a point of looking at the figures really closely. When you get up close to them, you can make out the cracks and wrinkles in the paintwork, the exaggeration in their features. I think perhaps I looked at them too hard because I keep seeing their faces all the time now. Sometimes, when I'm walking back to the caravan, I see their glazed eyes staring at me in the dark and, in the seconds when I've closed my eyes before I go to sleep, I see this parade of haunted faces and twisted features. Sometimes they seem so real that I could almost reach out and touch the decaying dampness of their skin.

I remember once visiting a waxworks when I was a kid. I think it was Madame Tussaud's. I'd seen it advertised on the telly and I kept going on at my mum and dad to take me. There were all these models of famous TV stars there. I was really disappointed. None of them looked real. And, when I went in the Chamber of Horrors, that didn't look real either. It certainly wasn't scary. I couldn't decide what was wrong at first, but then, afterwards, when we were outside waiting for a bus I found myself noticing the mannequins in the shop windows. That's when I realized for the first time that nobody ever stands still. Nobody stands completely motionless. Everybody moves. That's what was wrong with the models. They were standing perfectly still, so still that no one could ever imagine they were real.

That's why I feel uncomfortable when I'm working in the castle. Because none of the models are supposed to be alive. All of them are dead. And that's just how they look, you see – life-like but dead. It's the stillness of them that makes them seem so spooky. The soundlessness. It's the hanging silence in the empty hall and the frozen eyes that pierce into the back of my neck whenever I turn around and try to get on with my work.

Anyway, enough of that. The weather's brightened up at the moment so they've set us on painting the outside. We've been busy erecting scaffolding around the castle so that we can *paint it top to bottom. They do it every year. It's a bit chilly at the moment but it still feels good to be outside in the fresh air.*

What seems strange now is the year when I was on the dole when I used to stay in bed till lunchtime. I told myself it was good because it saved on the heating bills. I've got a lot more energy now and I'm up every morning at seven. I still have a lie-in on Sundays though.

You asked me whether I'd been making any friends. Not many. I get on all right with the blokes I work with but they nearly all live fairly close so they tend to go home at night. Or at the week-end anyway. If it was girls you were thinking of, well the only female I've been chatting to is an old woman who comes down to the lakeside and feeds the ducks. I talk to her sometimes while I eat my sarnies if I'm working on my own. She told me how she used to be a schoolteacher until it suddenly dawned on her one day that she couldn't stand the kids. That's not surprising. I remember some of the things we used to get up to with our teachers when we were at school.

That's all for now, anyway. I'll be back in three weeks' time for Christmas. It'll be smashing to see you again. I am missing you, you know.

Lots of love,

Wayne

NIGHTMARE PARK

A JOURNEY
INTO *FEAR*

Nightmare Park
Thursday

Dear Vi,

Well, here I am back at work. It was lovely to see you over
Christmas but, do you know, I'm missing you already? That
Snoopy hot-water bottle you bought me might be warm and
cuddly but it isn't exactly a substitute for you. Still, I suppose
it'll have to do for the time being. I don't think anyone could
have bought me a better present. It's freezing here in the
caravan. I'm sitting right up close to the calor gas stove whilst
I write this letter but my hands are so cold they can hardly
hold the pen.

Tell your mum and dad that I'm very grateful as well for
the scarf and woolly hat. Trust your dad to remember that I
support Sheffield United. I'm wearing the hat and scarf all
day because I'm working outside all the time now. Although
it's cold, it's fine and sunny so we've started painting the
castle. I'm working right at the top on the scaffolding. I was a
bit scared at first with it being so high up. I kept worrying
that I might forget where I was and step backwards and fall
off, but of course you never do anything so stupid. I don't
worry about it now – even though I can't swim (I haven't
mentioned that to anyone – they'd think I was really stupid!)
and the scaffolding overlooks the artificial lake.

I wish you could see the lake. It's beautiful. For a sort of
back-drop, it has this hill with lots of tall trees and then
Dracula's castle perched upon the top. There's a huge
Corkscrew ride called Satan's Staircase that comes round the
side of the castle and then drops right down and disappears
underneath the lake – it goes through a long dark tunnel and

22

out the other side. I've not been on it of course, because everything's closed for the winter but it sounds amazing – it must have been a fantastic job for them to build. Anyway, I was telling you about the lake – it's quite big with an island in the middle and it always seems to be still – even when it's windy in other places. I suppose that's because it's sheltered by the trees and by the hill.

What makes the lake look really spooky is that sometimes you get this mist, sort of rising and floating just above the water – it looks really weird. In the season, apparently, they have people dressed up as ghosts to take customers across on gondolas to the Gingerbread House on the island. I can't wait to see them. In fact, I'm wondering if I couldn't get a job here in the summer – how would you like to be able to tell your friends that your boyfriend was a ghost????

Lots of love,

Wayne

NIGHTMARE PARK

A JOURNEY
INTO *FEAR*

Nightmare Park
Saturday

Dear Vi,

Thank you very much for your letter. It really cheered
me up when you said you might be able to come over for
the day. It would be smashing to see you as I've been
feeling really lonely. I still haven't made any friends.
There's nothing wrong with the other blokes – they're all
okay. They're just older than me and they all knew one
another before I arrived which makes me a bit of an
outsider.

Did I tell you about the old woman I met as well? At
first I thought she was mad – I'm not so sure now –
maybe, she's just a bit strange. She always has this massive
shopping bag. It just occurred to me the other day that
there aren't any shops for miles around so I wondered what
she kept in it. I mean, she brings bread for the ducks but
she could carry a few crusts of bread in her pocket.
Anyway, I just had a peek one day last week while she was
standing at the water's edge – and it's her tool box. It's full
of adjustable spanners and wrenches and screwdrivers and
things. You just don't think of an old lady carrying a tool
bag around with her, do you? It turns out that she lives
inside the Gingerbread House – she must be some kind of
caretaker or something and she looks after it and fixes
everything. It's true what my mum and dad said – you
meet all sorts of people when you start work.

24

You didn't tell me much about yourself and what you've been doing. I do like to get some news about what's happening at home, you know. Write back soon.

Love,

Wayne

Dear Vi,

I'm sorry to have to write about this and I don't want to
seem suspicious but I had a letter from Bob last week and he
mentioned about how you'd been seeing some other bloke.
It's been on my mind so much that I thought I'd better write
and try to clear things up. It might not be true of course and I
don't want you to think I'm the sort of bloke that gets really
jealous because it's not that I'm possessive, it's just that I need
to know.

So, is it true that you've been going out with Jordan
Thorpe? As I say, I don't want to seem suspicious but, if it is
true Vi, it would have been better if you'd told me about it
yourself instead of hearing it from my brother. Anyway is it
serious or not? I suppose I've got to know.

See you then,

Wayne

NIGHTMARE PARK

A JOURNEY
INTO *FEAR*

Nightmare Park

Dear Vi,

Well, it looks like that's it then, doesn't it? I mean, I don't know what you expected me to say. I mean, I don't know what else I can do.

I mean, it seems a shame because I'm earning a lot of money now and I could afford to take you out and everything which I couldn't do before. I was even thinking we could have gone away together for the week-end or had a bit of a holiday or something. Anyway, it doesn't matter but I think you could have waited a bit longer than you did.

I've been thinking things over and what I've decided now is that I might stay on here over the season. The place is getting busier and everything's brightening up — there doesn't seem so much point in me coming back home now and, if I can get work here for the summer, I think it would be best for me to stay. I was talking to Agnes the other day — the old lady who lives in the Gingerbread House. She's asked me to go over there this afternoon — she says there might be some extra jobs that I could do for her.

Anyway, I'll see you around when I get back. I'm sorry things had to finish like this. I'd like to have been able to see you and have a chat about it instead of having to try and explain everything in a letter. I never was much good at writing.

All the best anyway.

Wayne

27

Nightmare youth vanishes

Police are investigating the mysterious disappearance of a young trainee, Wayne Gate, who was last seen working on the exterior paintwork of *Dracula's Castle* at Nightmare Park.

Seventeen-year-old Wayne, who had previously been unemployed for twelve months, had recently started his first ever job as a trainee at the new amusement park. He was well-liked by his workmates who described him as a 'quiet, likeable lad, not one to mess about.' Wayne's girlfriend, Violet Bank, had recently finished their relationship but said that Wayne did not seem unduly depressed.

Fears are that Wayne may have had an accident and fallen from high scaffolding whilst painting the park's famous *Dracula's Castle*.

Nightmare Park safety officer, David Sharrow, said in a statement today: 'We are very much concerned about Wayne's disappearance. Nightmare Park has extremely high safety standards and we take very good care of all our young trainees. I cannot believe that he has had an accident of any sort.'

Police are continuing their investigations.

'Have you seen this?'

Marie passes me the newspaper with the article about Nightmare Park. 'I wonder what's happened to this Wayne,' she says excitedly. 'I bet he didn't just fall off the scaffolding.'

'Why not?'

'Well, people don't, do they? I mean, how many times have you walked past a piece of scaffolding and seen painters and builders and people flying over the edge?'

I think about it and start to grin. 'I know, but . . .'

'I bet something horrible's happened to him. I bet he's been squashed underneath the roller coaster or fallen upside down out of the Corkscrew ride. The people who own the park won't let on because they don't want to lose any customers. They're always claiming how safe it is.'

'People don't fall off Corkscrews either,' I tell her. 'They wouldn't be allowed to build them if people could fall off.'

'Well, what about that really fat woman in America?'

I've heard Marie tell this story before.

'She just shot off the roller coaster at *Magic Mountain* when it got to the bottom of a drop. She was enormous. You see, she was so fat that her gravitational pull was greater than the centrifugal force.'

'Sorry I'm late.' A tall, slim woman dressed in yellow scurries into the classroom, almost hidden by armfuls of books.

Marie lowers her voice and carries on. 'And did you hear about those men that got beheaded?'

I nod. I don't really want to hear all the gory details but as

29

Marie huddles over whispering right into my earhole, it isn't easy to avoid.

The woman spills the books, some of them onto the teacher's desk and some of them onto the floor. Bernadette Dronfield goes out to help her pick them up.

'They made the mistake of standing up, you see. Now, you must never stand up on a roller coaster.'

I nod. The only time I went on a roller coaster I felt like fainting or being sick. The last thing I felt like was standing up.

'Somebody had a bet with them that they wouldn't dare stand up. What they didn't realize was that there was this metal bar across the track. They went past with such force that it just sliced their heads right off. I mean, can you imagine, standing waiting for a ride and when the car comes round the corner it's got these . . .'

'Good morning.' The tall, yellow woman stands and faces the class, forcing a smile. Hardly anyone has noticed so most of the class just carry on talking.

Marie passes the newspaper to Tony and Jez. 'Have you seen this article about Nightmare Park?' she asks them. 'I think this boy's got killed.' She points out the paragraph. 'Did I tell you about those blokes that got beheaded on a roller coaster. . . ?'

'When you're ready . . .' The new teacher is beginning to sound impatient. People stop talking and look at her, most of them for the first time.

'My name is Ms Maltby and I shall be taking you for Media Studies until half-term.'

There's a pause.

I can see Marie's face breaking into an evil smirk. I try not to look at her because, if I do, the chances are that I'll break out into giggles.

Ms Maltby is dressed completely in yellow. She has a yellow blouse, yellow straight skirt, yellow shoes and tights;

she even has a yellow ribbon in her hair. Someone at the back of the class starts humming *Tie a Yellow Ribbon round the Old Oak Tree*.

Tony puts his hand up. 'Are you a student, Miss?'

We have a riot with students. Anticipation starts to build up around the class. Someone else starts singing the tune to *Goldfinger*.

Ms Maltby hesitates. She scans the groups of grinning faces. She's beginning to look less sure of herself. 'Yes,' she nods. 'I'm from the Institute of Education.' She scowls at Jez who's just started whistling the tune to *The Yellow Rose of Texas*.

Last time we had a student we superglued her chalk down to the blackboard, invited a neighbour's child into our class from a completely different school during their half-term break, and sneaked an inflatable whoopee cushion onto her chair whilst she was in the stockroom looking for extra chalk. And that was just in the first lesson.

A low and subtle cacophony is starting up as everyone thinks of songs that have something to do with yellow in the title.

Ms Maltby starts looking more worried. 'I thought you might find it interesting to do some work on video and scriptwriting.'

Marie points her lips into an 'Oooh! Isn't this exciting' expression and turns around so that everyone in the class can see. Within seconds, all the others are nodding with an evil enthusiasm.

Ms Maltby looks slightly suspicious. She swallows hard. 'Right then.'

Marie puts her hand up.

'Yes?'

'Would you like me to give the books out, Miss?'

'That's very kind of you.'

Marie leaps forward and grabs the pile of books. I know

she'll do something awful, like dropping them all on the floor.

'Now what do you know about video and scriptwriting?'

Everyone's looking expectantly at Marie. What she does, in fact, is to give the books out quietly but give them to all the wrong people. She scrutinizes the names on the covers but then gives every book to someone at the opposite corner of the class.

Within two or three minutes there's chaos. People start clambering out of their places and walking around to find their books; others throw books across the classroom, shouting out the name of the person they're aimed at. The only books that Marie gives out to their rightful owners are hers and mine. She sits down struggling to keep a straight face as the classroom disintegrates into anarchy.

After school Marie wants to go back to the classroom to pick up her English book. 'I'm working on my story,' she tells me. 'It's going to be really good.'

This story is supposed to be like a short novel. We've got all term to finish it so I don't know what the hurry is, but I go back with her anyway and wait for her to find her book.

As we walk into the classroom, we can see Ms Maltby's bag left out on the teacher's desk. There's a flash of yellow from inside the stockroom and then the stockroom door slams shut. Marie starts singing *We all live in a Yellow Submarine* but I don't think Ms Maltby can hear. There's a brass band practice next door and the walls are pretty thin.

Marie takes her English book out of her locker and puts it in her bag. 'Hey,' she says to me. 'Do you know which class has music on Wednesday afternoon?'

I shake my head. 'Is it 4N?' I ask her. I don't really know.

'We could tell them to ask their teacher for different songs – like *Yellow Submarine*.

32

Ms Maltby was getting really fed up with the yellow songs by the end of the afternoon. I can just imagine her reaction if they were actually coming from the next door.

I grin. Or *'Mellow Yellow.'*

Marie picks up her bag and then stops in her tracks staring at the stockroom door.

'What's the matter?'

She has a mischievous look in her eye. 'The door. Look,' she whispers. 'The keys are in the door.'

Oh no. I look at the bunch of keys and straightaway I know what Marie is thinking. I shake my head. 'She'd hear them,' I whisper.

'Not in there. Not with the band playing.'

She could be right. Between our classroom and the music room is a walk-in cupboard where the cleaners keep their mops and buckets. The band sounds really loud even though the cupboard is between us. The stockroom is at the back, so it juts right into the music room. The band must be almost deafening in there.

Marie is already collapsing into giggles of excitement. She scans around the classroom. 'Check there's nobody coming,' she whispers.

'No,' I tell her. 'You mustn't.' But I don't sound very persuasive.

'Go on.'

I open the door and peer out into the corridor. There's no one there. 'It's okay.'

I can't really believe she's going to do it but, when I turn round, Marie is already tiptoeing over to the stockroom. She checks out of the window to make sure there's no one watching. She reaches tentatively towards the keys then snatches back her hand and clasps it over her mouth to keep the giggles from escaping. 'Hurry up,' I whisper but Marie can't hear me.

I stand by the half-open door and peep out into the

corridor. If anyone comes in and sees us, then we've had it. We'd both get caught red-handed.

She reaches out again and this time her fingers touch the keys. I'm terrified they're going to clatter; I'm scared she's going to drop them. In my mind I do the actions with her. I feel the metal in my hand. I feel it start to move. My heart jumps as I see the key turn in the door. The sound's too slight to hear above the band. Marie has all the bunch of keys inside her hand. Now she lets go of them very, very cautiously, to make sure they don't make a noise. Hurry up.

I glance into the corridor again. There's still no one about. I swallow hard. Come on.

Marie lets go of the keys and tiptoes across the classroom floor. She grabs me round the waist and silently whoops up into the air. Both of us crease ourselves, the suppressed laughter leaking out as muffled sniggers, then we dash out of the classroom. We run down the corridor and round the corner; we can't wait to get outside and just explode.

'Don't. Don't run,' Marie warns me as we see Bernadette Dronfield walking out of the girls' toilets. She'll have stayed late for the band practice. 'Hi,' chokes Marie.

'Hi,' says Bernadette. She obviously wonders what we've been up to. 'You're late.'

'We had to come back for something,' Marie calls over her shoulder as we disappear down the corridor.

We walk sedately out of the foyer and round the back of the school past the CDT block out of sight before we sit on the grass and explode.

*

It's several minutes later before Marie realizes that she's left her bag inside the classroom. 'Oh no,' she says. She closes her eyes for a moment and lets out her breath. 'I'll have to go back for it.'

34

I hope she's not expecting me to go back with her. 'Why will you?'

She thinks about it. 'It'll look suspicious, won't it? When somebody lets her out . . . I mean, if the first thing she sees is my bag . . .'

'Mmmm. She might remember that it wasn't there before.'

'Hey.' Marie starts laughing again. 'Do you think somebody will let her out?'

'The caretaker will, won't she? Or the cleaners?'

'I should think so.'

I start to giggle as well. 'Hey, it'll be funny if she's there all night.'

'Can you imagine at registration tomorrow morning?' Marie does a high-pitched imitation of Ms Maltby's voice: *'Hello. Is there anybody there? It's Mellow Yellow.'*

We both laugh out loud again.

'Oh dear.' Marie shakes her head. 'What are we going to do about my bag, though?'

'Do you think she'll still be locked in?'

'I don't know.'

There's an uneasy silence whilst both of us think what to do. 'Let's walk across the field,' says Marie. 'We might be able to see something.'

Our classroom looks out over the playing fields. 'What if she looks outside and sees us?'

'Well, we're only going home, aren't we? There's nothing wrong with that.'

'Okay.'

We set off walking across the field but, as soon as our classroom comes into sight, I can see the patch of yellow waving at the window like a gigantic netted butterfly.

'Oh no.'

'What?'

I'm talking through my clenched teeth but I don't know

why. There's no one around to hear us. 'Don't look,' I tell her. 'She's standing there at the window.'

'Are you sure?'

'You can't miss her.'

'Oh no.' Marie glances across. 'It's like the Yellow Peril.'

'Shall we go back?'

'No. She'll have seen us.'

Marie grabs hold of my arm. 'Don't turn round,' I tell her. 'Keep looking straight in front.'

But Marie just can't contain herself. At first she glances out of the corner of her eye, but then she just stands and stares.

'Come on.' I try and pull her away.

'She's waving her arms like a windmill,' says Marie. 'Let's go and ask her what's the matter?'

'We can't!'

''Course we can. She'll be really embarrassed.'

I sigh. Already, Marie is setting her face into an *Oh dear, I think there's something the matter with our teacher. Is there anything we can do to help?* expression and setting off over to the classroom. I shake my head and walk behind.

It's about ten minutes later before we finally rescue Ms Maltby. What makes it all really embarrassing is that she's so extremely grateful. Apparently, she suffers from claustrophobia and, if she's ever locked in a confined space, she goes into an absolute panic. Another few seconds and she might have had a heart attack.

'It's such a good job you came past,' she gasps, fluttering out of the stockroom. 'I don't know what I'd have done. I really don't.' She shakes her head as she looks around the room. 'I suppose it must have been the caretaker that came and turned the keys, but you'd think she'd have checked there was nobody inside.'

'They make a lot of noise next door,' I volunteer. 'If she knocked you might not have heard her.'

'Mmmm.' Ms Maltby looks thoughtful. 'Well, I really am grateful to you,' she says. 'I shall get you a present – both of you. I don't know what it'll be but . . . I shall buy you something.'

'Oh, there's no need . . .' I start to say but Marie just smiles with a look of total innocence. 'That's very kind of you, Ms Maltby,' she says. 'Very kind indeed.'

Next morning in Assembly, Sister Frances decides to find the culprit. Ours is a Catholic school and that's why we have a nun for the headmistress. Marie calls her a witch. She calls her a witch because she has a long hooked nose, big warts on her face and she eats teenagers for breakfast.

First of all she stands in the centre of the stage, directly below the big silver crucifix on the wall and stares around the room, moving her head slowly to achieve maximum eye contact with everyone. All those who've done anything wrong in the last twenty four hours – and that's most people really, when you think about it – lower their eyes to the floor. Along with the Stare comes the Silence. Whilst Sister Frances is staring every one of us in the eyes, she never says a word. She just looks. A terrible ominous pressure builds up round the room.

Then she starts to speak. Sister never starts by telling us what's happened; she leaves that until the end. She gives the sermon first. If she gives a sermon on dishonesty, for instance, anybody who's borrowed something in the last few weeks and forgotten to give it back starts to curl up with guilt and embarrassment. Then, when she mentions what the actual crime is, you can see people starting to relax.

Today's sermon is on the subject of fear. She talks about our rational fears, about our fear of evil and fear of the unknown and then she tells us about irrational fears or phobias. I can feel myself starting to go cherry red. I just daren't look at Marie. Sister Frances goes on about how terrible it must be to suffer from a phobia and tells us to imagine what it must be like to be afraid of the dark or terrified of confined spaces. I start feeling weak and faint. I hope I don't collapse. 'Would you believe,' asks Sister Frances, speaking slowly for the maximum effect, 'would you believe that there is someone in this school who could actually take a perverse delight in locking someone with claustrophobia in a school stockroom?'

There's a stunned, shocked silence. Sister stares at the rows of horrified, unbelieving faces. 'And would you believe that this was done to a *visitor*' – she says the word, 'visitor' the way most people say 'prime minister'.

Some of the first years gasp out loud.

I think it's unfair because we didn't actually know that Mellow Yellow was claustrophobic.

'I think,' Sister says, gazing round, 'I think there is somebody in this room who can help us.'

'Here we go,' Marie mutters in between her clenched teeth. 'Bring on the snitches.'

Sister has these long dark hairs that stick out of her warts. Marie calls them her antennae. When she senses evil, the hairs start to tremble and quiver. I can tell that they're quivering now, even though we're standing several rows back. I see them sticking out as Sister stares around the room.

'I think that someone in this school saw people waiting round Room 14 late yesterday afternoon.' She pauses. 'I think there is at least one person here in this hall who has suspicions about who the culprit might be.'

I can see Bernadette Dronfield standing a few rows in front of us. I wonder if she's thinking about when she saw us both last night. I start to feel sick.

'And, believe me, I shall find out.' Sister Frances looks up and down the rows of cowering faces. 'I shall find out very soon.' She pauses. 'I shall expect the culprit . . . or culprits . . . to come and see me sometime this morning.'

My stomach turns over in panic at the very thought.

She points her finger towards the row where Marie and I are standing. I shiver as her eyes bore into my head. The tone of her voice is formidable. 'I shall expect them to come and see me before . . .' she gazes steadily around the hall for the last time . . . 'before I have to come and see them.'

*

My legs are trembling as I stagger out into the corridor. I tell myself I have to keep upright; it'll look suspicious if I faint. I daren't look around at anyone else in case they've noticed the state I'm in.

I wait until we get inside the classroom and I can whisper in the corner to Marie. 'What are we going to do?' I ask her.

Marie just shakes her head.

'She's bound to find out.'

'I don't know.'

'She always finds out.'

Marie makes a desperate attempt to make me laugh. She points her finger at me then gives a cackling imitation of Sister Frances. 'If you do not confess, my girl, you will be turned into a frog this very night.'

I smile but I can't really find it funny.

Marie contorts her face into a maniacal leer. 'You will grow warts on your face like mine and your nose will grow into a massive beak.'

'It's not funny,' I say, still managing to chuckle. 'What are we going to do?'

Marie just shakes her head. 'We can't do anything.'

I keep thinking of Sister's words: *I shall expect them to come and see me before I have to come and see them*. I have a feeling of terrible dread, like a black vulture wrapped around my rib cage.

'She always says how she'll find out,' Marie scoffs. 'She never does.'

'Yes, she does,' I argue. 'She solves crimes before anyone's even done them.'

'Only because people run to her and confess. If people just waited and kept quiet, she'd never find out anything at all.'

Halfway through the lesson, a second year comes round with a note: *Please will anyone who stayed behind after school last night go to see Sister Frances straightaway*.

I feel my heart lurch over. This must be it. I don't know whether Marie and I ought to go or not. I look across at

Marie but she's buried herself inside *Testament of Youth* like a hibernating tortoise.

Three or four people, those who stayed last night for the band practice and for gym club, start heading towards the door. Bernadette Dronfield goes with them.

My stomach somersaults with dread. We're doomed. I don't know what we're going to do. I imagine the second year coming back and calling out my name; I think of walking beside her down the corridor then staggering into Sister's office, trying not to cry. Oh God, I hope I don't cry. I think of them all sitting in a circle round me, the gym club and the band and Sister Frances and Mellow Yellow. I imagine Bernadette Dronfield pointing her finger at me. The perspiration is standing out on my forehead. I don't know what to do.

I usually go to Marie's house one night a week. When we've had English homework I often take my book with me and let Marie have a look. She's very very good at English. She doesn't do the work for me – she just checks it through and corrects my spelling mistakes and punctuation – things like that.

Marie lives at Hartley Grange, over twenty minutes' bus ride from our house. I often think if anybody were to see Marie's house and ours standing side by side, they'd find it impossible to believe that we were best friends. Our families couldn't be any more different. Our house is tiny and overcrowded with rows of washing – baby vests, nighties and pants drying by the heater. Everywhere is noise and steam. Paul and Carmel are nearly always quarrelling, cartoons and quiz shows are turned up high on the television, the budgie chatters away and there are pans boiling, pots clattering, the washer rumbling and all kinds of toys squeaking and rolling about the floor.

I don't know what my mum would think if she ever saw the inside of *The Grange*. Everything there is vast and silent. It's more like a library than a house. Or like living inside the Town Hall. There are shelves and shelves of books and wooden floorboards with Chinese rugs. I don't know why Marie's parents don't buy carpets. They could easily afford them. I go up there on the number twenty seven and then I walk down Hartley Grange Road and I hardly ever see anyone at all – not walking anyway. You sometimes see big cars turning into the driveways. The houses are set so far back that all you can see are pointed roofs peering over the trees like mountain tops.

I turn and walk down the Millhouse's driveway. I always feel a bit nervous even though I've been coming here about once a week for nearly a year now. I think what I still remember is the nervousness I felt the first time I was invited. I thought I must have made a mistake and got the wrong address. I thought that when the people opened the door, they'd send me away. But of course they didn't. I don't see much of Marie's mum and dad, but when I do, they're very nice to me. Of course, I always look smart when I come. I always have my shoes polished and make sure my socks are nice and clean. I don't want to show myself up.

Marie's house has two front doors. I open the first one and stand inside a little porch that has a tiled floor and rows of shelves that are filled with potted plants. Then I press the bell on the inside door and wait for Marie to let me in. We don't have a bell at our house. People just knock on the door and walk inside shouting, 'Hello! Is there anybody in? It's only me.' Or something like that. The only person who stands on the step and waits is the man from the Prudential.

Marie opens the door and grins. 'Hi!' she says. 'Come in.'

I follow her into the hall. It has panels of polished wood and a case on the wall that operates the burglar alarm. Marie takes my coat and goes to hang it in the cloakroom. Before I came here, I thought you only had cloakrooms in schools and churches and places like that. Marie's cloakroom isn't just a place to put your clothes – it has a toilet and a washbasin as well.

Then we go upstairs to Marie's bedroom. It ought to be really beautiful because it's right at the top of the house inside the roof and it stretches across with big dormer windows on either side. If you look one way, you can see right into the centre of the city; through the other window you can see the countryside.

Standing by the long wall are fitted units with a desk and stacking systems for Marie's hi-fi, colour TV, cassette deck and, of course rows and rows of books. I say that the bedroom *ought to* be beautiful because what I don't think many people would like is Marie's style in decorations. Everything is to do with ghosts and vampires, witches or werewolves. She has a Dracula mobile over her bed, posters from horror films with rats and other overgrown monsters and a reading lamp she's made herself which has pictures of spooky things stuck on so the light shines through them when you switch the red bulb on. It made me shudder the first time I came to visit but I'm getting more used to it now.

'Well, we're still alive,' Marie says, taking out her English book.

'Yes.' I've never prayed so much in one day in the whole of my life. 'Do you think we're going to be all right?' I ask Marie.

She looks thoughtful. 'I thought we'd had it when Sister sent for all the kids who'd stayed to gym and band practice, but then . . . well, if anyone saw us . . . like Bernadette . . . well, we admitted being there, didn't we? We said we'd gone to fetch my book and then to let Mellow Yellow out.'

'Don't you think she suspected?'

Marie shakes her head. 'She wouldn't have offered to buy us both a present each, would she?'

'Look, we can't let her . . .'

'Why not?' she grins. 'I wonder what it'll be.'

I sit down on the padded seat below Marie's window and look out over the town. I think about my mum and how proud she is of me doing well at school. She'd go berserk if I got into trouble and had to be expelled.

'I've just been finishing my story.' Marie says, picking up her English book.

'Finishing it?'

'Mmmmm.'

'But we've got all term to do it.'

'That doesn't mean you're not allowed to finish early.'

'I know but . . .'

'Don't you want to have a look at it?'

'Of course I do.' Marie's stories are always really good. I don't know where she gets her ideas from. 'What's it about?'

'Well, I'll tell you,' Marie says. 'I'll just explain about the first part. Are you sitting comfortably?'

'Yes, thank you.'

'Here's another cushion.' She throws a bean bag at me. It lands straight on my head.

'I said I *was* comfortable.'

'Okay then, here we go.' Marie opens her book.

I put the bean bag underneath me and listen.

'Right, well, the story is about two girls called Hazel and Kimberley who live in a children's home. . . . It's like a prison for teenagers.

'This place is right out in the country. Hazel and Kimberley decide to escape and when they do they hide all day, then, when it's starting to get dark, they go down to the nearest village and try and steal some food.'

'Won't the police be looking for them?'

'Well, that's it, you see, because they are. The woman in the shop where they go, she telephones the police and so the two girls run into the country and hide. Only there isn't anywhere much to hide. I mean, there aren't any woods or derelict buildings and the country is all flat. It's really cold and wet and muddy as well. So, when they see the police cars touring up and down looking for them, they just have to crouch behind these really scraggy bushes in the mud.'

'It sounds horrible. I think I'd just give myself up.'

'Well, one of the girls – that's Kimberley – she's like that.

45

I mean she's really weak and snivelling and scared and she just wants to go back to the home and drink her cocoa and go to bed, but the other one – that's Hazel – she's got more about her. I mean, she's a lot stronger. "We'll go back over my dead body," she says.'

'That sounds ominous.'

'Yes, well, it's supposed to be.'

I notice that these two girls sound rather like Marie and me – or the way that Marie seems to think of us. She always thinks of herself as really tough. Even though I've known her such a long time, I can't make up my mind whether she's really like that or whether it's all a big act she puts on.

'So, what do they do then?' I ask her.

'Right. Well, they're both ever so cold and wet and fed up and then they come to this really high wire fence. At first it looks like the sort of fence they have around an R.A.F. camp or something. Or a big factory with guard dogs. Everything's really dark. They can't see what's inside the fence. So, they climb right over the top and then they're at the back of the buildings so they can't see what they are. There's a little doorway in the first one, but it's locked. The girls are really exhausted now and their feet keep sinking down into the mud, so they just stagger – or squelch – over to the next building and the door's shut there – but they think they can force it open. Well, they don't actually break the door; they just kind of squeeze in through an opening at the bottom. That's quite important to the story because it means that nobody can find where they've gone; they haven't left any tracks or anything.'

'I see.'

'So, they just squeeze inside all wet and muddy and exhausted and collapse onto this sort of wooden crate and drink their cans of coke that they've stolen from the shop.

'I'll just read you a bit now. This is the part where they've finished their drinks and Hazel starts to explore.'

'Okay.' I curl up on the bean bag with my arms wrapped round my knees.

'You might find this a bit frightening,' Marie explains, 'but just remember, that it is only a story.'

'I'll try and remember.'

'Although it is very realistic.'

'Right.'

Marie finds the place and starts to read:

Kimberley shivered. She felt as if the cold went right through to her inside; she didn't know how they were going to get warm enough to sleep. For the first time she looked around her and tried to make out objects in the dark. 'I wonder where we are,' she said.

'There's another of these wooden boxes over there – I'll just have a look.' Hazel moved across.

'Don't go away.' Kimberley's voice betrayed her panic. She was terrified of being left on her own. But as well as that, there was something else. Something she couldn't even give voice to. A shape of something she was just trying to make out in the dark. She opened her mouth and then closed it; her lips were moving and her teeth were chattering but no other sound would come out. She was speechless. She was trying to see in the dark. There was no moonlight, no window, nothing to see by and yet in front of her was a shape. There was no mistake about it. It was about four or five metres away from her and the size of a very tall man. It was wearing a kind of long white sheet and it was glowing, shining in the dark. Kimberley nearly fainted. There could be no doubt about it. It was a ghost.

Kimberley stared open-mouthed at the shape. She tried to call Hazel again but still no words would come so she leapt across and grabbed her by the arm. Hazel was opening the box, the long dark wooden box that was just like the one they'd been sitting on. As Kimberley touched Hazel's arm, the lid of the box was half-open. Hazel's arm went rigid. She was staring inside the box. Her eyes were glazed with terror. Kimberley looked and felt the blood drain from her face. Her knees buckled as she almost collapsed with shock. The boxes weren't just wooden crates. Why hadn't they noticed the shape of them before? They were so distinct. They weren't wooden crates; they were coffins. And there in the coffin in front of them, lying staring upwards with its sunken eyes and sneering at them with its hollow toothy grin was the grey, decaying structure of a skeleton.

Kimberley let out a scream. She was shaking with terror. Hazel held her hand over Kimberley's mouth. 'Don't,' she told her. 'They'll hear us.'

Kimberley wanted to run, to escape, but she was rooted to the spot. All she could feel was fear. She stared at the coffin, transfixed, her heart pounding.

'Come on.' Hazel pulled Kimberley back away from the apparition. 'Come on.' Hazel pulled urgently on Kimberley's arm. 'Don't look. Just come away.'

The two girls staggered backwards clinging on to each other. 'Hold on to me. Don't let go,' said Hazel.

They came to a door. It looked like a cupboard. Hazel began to push it open.

'Don't.' Kimberley almost screamed. She was terrified. They didn't know what might be inside. But already Hazel had opened the door.

'Well, what do you think of it so far?' Marie looks at me over the top of her book.

'It's brill.'

'You're not finding it too frightening?'

'Well, a little bit, but I might survive.'

'Do you want to know what they find inside the door?' Marie asks me.

'I can't wait.'

'I was just going to make a cup of coffee.'

'OK.'

'Do you want one?'

'I'll have to be careful I don't spill it. I mean, my hands'll be shaking so much.'

Marie walks across and plugs her kettle in. 'Do you really like it then?' she asks me.

'I think it's great, but I mean, where are they? I can't understand what's happened to them. It's not like a graveyard or anything.'

'I thought you might have guessed.'

I shake my head.

Marie spoons the coffee out into the mugs. 'I'm letting you have my Winnie the Pooh mug today,' she tells me.

'Oh Wow!'

'That's just because you like my story.'

She waits for the kettle to boil then makes the coffee. She comes back and sits down and passes me Winnie the Pooh.

'Right,' she says, 'I'll explain. It's a big amusement park – in fact, it's Nightmare Park. What they've done is to get inside one of the rides – like the *Dracula's Castle*, but because they've gone in from the back, they don't understand where they are.'

'I see. What happens next then?'

'Right, well the room they go into is the control room where all the switches are, although they don't realize that of course. And there's this rail that goes right through it. I'll read you about the control room.'

'OK.'

'There ought to be some heating,' Hazel said, looking at the rows of switches.

The switches all had labels but none of them made much sense. 'What about CIRCULATE?' said Kimberley. 'That might be for the heating system.'

49

'Mmmm. Or perhaps we should try ACTIVATE.' Hazel pressed down the first two switches. 'We'll have them both.'

There was an instant whirring and clattering, like a heavy motor being started up. 'Well, something's happening,' said Hazel. It sounded like the start of a big dipper at the fair, the first part, when the cars go up the slope, pulled by a massive chain. 'I hope nobody can hear it from outside.'

The clattering sound was getting louder. 'It seems a funny sort of heating system.'

'I don't think it's . . .' Kimberley started. But then she stopped. The sound seemed to be coming from the wall right next to them. It was just as though a clumsy great machine was about to burst through the wall of the office.

The girls stared at each other in horror. When the thing came, it was not a machine; it was Dracula. Dracula actually came through the wall of the office. Hazel backed to the door and reached behind her for the handle. She couldn't work out what was going on, but whatever it was, she wanted to get out. Dracula came gliding past only two or three metres away. Hazel groped round the door. She couldn't believe it: there wasn't a handle on the inside. They were both locked in.

'Oh no,' she screamed. 'Help!' She battered on the wooden door.

'Come on. Open the door!' sobbed Kimberley.

'I can't. We're locked in!'

They heard the sound of clattering once again. 'Oh no!' screamed Hazel. 'There's something else.'

The two girls stood, trembling, staring at the wall waiting for what would happen next. The clattering came nearer and nearer; but all Kimberley could do was laugh. Hazel was staring at the hole in the wall waiting for the apparition. When it came, it was a woman, a female Vampire. She was tall and slim and wearing a long white robe that stretched almost to the floor. She had jet black hair that hung straight

50

down to her waist. Her face was deathly white with heavy black make-up round her eyes and crimson red lips, parted in a sneer that showed her blood-soaked fangs.

Hazel shuddered as Kimberley huddled beside her, laughing out loud again. As the woman passed out of the room, Hazel noticed that her feet were wedged into a square kind of tin box that was fastened to the rail.

As she stood and stared in silence and disbelief, she saw another two tin boxes glide past. Both of them were empty. She walked across to the wall and turned off the two switches. The motor and the clattering stopped.

Hazel stood and thought. She frowned. 'None of these things can be real,' she said. 'They're all mechanical. It must be . . . like some kind of a film set or . . . like some kind of ride at a fair. It'll be closed down now for the winter. That's why there's nobody about.' She paused. 'The only way out is through the hole in the wall with the monsters. We'll just have to follow them . . .'

Kimberley just stared at the space in the wall. And Hazel went on. 'Look, there'll be some more of those spare boxes on the rail – that's what they stand up in. We can climb into those when they come past – then we'll just ride round with the monsters. We'll look out for a sensible place to jump off and we'll be alright.

'First we'll have to press the circulate lever again,' Hazel explained. 'And the other one as well. That'll mean some more monsters coming through, but . . .' She looked at Kimberley with concern. 'We'll know what to expect this time. We'll be ready for them.'

Kimberley just stared vacantly.

'We'll try and find two boxes together so we can both be next to each other. OK?'

She squeezed Kimberley's shoulder and smiled at her reassuringly. 'We'll be ghouls ourselves in a minute, won't we?'

Kimberley said nothing.

Hazel looked at her and shook her head. 'I'll switch the motor on again,' she said.

'I wonder what it'll be this time.' She smiled and tried to look brave. 'It might be a ghost or Frankenstein's monster . . .'

It was Wolfman. He burst through the opening in the wall like a gigantic hairy tree trunk. His body looked like that of a huge orangutan, covered in long dark hair. His arms, which were swinging, ape-like, by his sides, ended in enormous paws with wrinkled palms and long, horny claws but his face was that of a man. It was covered in long wild hair with a bushy beard that covered up most of his features but his eyes were round and staring, gloating when he saw the two girls huddled together. Kimberley shrank away, clinging hold of Hazel. 'It's alright,' said Hazel. 'It's not real. It's only made-up. Don't be frightened.'

But, just as she said that, Wolfman's head began to twitch mechanically. As he trundled past on the rail he raised his fist in the air and waved it at the girls. Kimberley screamed.

'Come on.' Hazel spoke to her sharply. 'Come on. We'll be out of here in a minute.' One of the empty metal boxes passed them on the rail then another. 'Get ready to jump.'

The two girls crouched by the side of the rail. 'Here we go!' shouted Hazel as the empty boxes came past. 'Ready, steady, jump!'

It was two months later when workmen opened up the House of Horrors *ready for the new season. To their surprise, they found the electric motor whirring and the procession of ghosts and horrors already trundling round the hidden track. They were also horrified to find two new grisly exhibits that had not existed before. On the track in between Wolfman and the Hunchback of Notre Dame were the corpses of two young girls wearing anoraks and jeans. They appeared to have been*

52

electrocuted. The girls were later identified as Hazel Barrow and Kimberley Street, two inmates who had absconded nine weeks previously from Moorcroft Assessment Centre.

At the post mortem, the coroner came to the conclusion that the girls had been instantly electrocuted when they climbed on to the rail, as they were both wearing worn out plimsolls which, the coroner assumed, would probably have been wet at the time. The boxes on the rail contained live electrical connections for wiring up the remaining monsters which had been sent away for repair.

A verdict of death by misadventure was recorded.

It's two days later before Sister Frances calls Marie's name out in Assembly.

And it's just when I'm starting to think that maybe we've got away with locking Mellow Yellow in the stockroom.

For the past three days, I've been living in a state of dread. Every time I glimpse that black habit gliding down the corridor, my stomach sinks as if I've fallen off a cliff. Every time the classroom door opens, my guts have shrivelled like an octopus under attack. It's when I first wake up in a morning that I hate it most. I wake up in bed from a lovely dream and the sun is shining and it's a day when anything nice can happen and then, during the process of waking up – of remembering who I am, what day it is, whether I have to go to school or not – the weight inside my guts wakes up as well. It starts to turn over and stretch and then bangs its head against my stomach. And the rest of the day is like living inside a cave – dark and oppressive, with black flitting shadows clad in strange robes, hovering everywhere I turn.

First of all, Sister Frances tells us off about the litter. 'The school tuck shop and the vendomat will both be closed until every shred of chocolate wrapper, every crisp packet and every paper carton is picked up from the school field.' She pauses. 'What kind of impression do you think it gives a visitor. . . ?'

Marie often says that Sister cares so much about what visitors think that you'd assume the school was built for them instead of for the kids.

'What on earth will they think when they see the school driveway covered in your waste products?'

One or two people giggle but they do it very quietly.

'Anyone who arrives late during the next ten days can join a litter collection squad at break. These will be supervised by prefects . . .'

Sister Frances is a great believer in punishment. Every single foot wrong, every step out of line, everything carries a penance. She has them all worked out inside her head.

She closes the huge black heavy Bible which is normally the signal for the end of Assembly. Then she pauses. 'Is Marie Millhouse here?' she asks.

I feel my legs sink under me. My body sags like a bean bag. I have to try hard not to faint.

Marie is sitting two rows in front of me but I can actually feel her wilting. She shakily raises her hand. When Sister doesn't see her, she staggers to her feet.

'Come to my room at break please.' She says it briskly and with efficiency and I hold my breath in horror. Then Sister picks up her Bible and turns and walks out of the hall.

We're not allowed to speak a word until we're outside in the corridor. I look across at Marie but her face is without expression. She just stares ahead like a zombie as she walks out of the hall.

Getting to see Sister Frances in her office is like reaching the heart of a castle. First of all, you have to pass through ranks of guards – in other words, prefects – lined up by the doors. When you've got through those, there are desks of typists and a secretary – all of whom demand to know your name and whether you've got an appointment.

Marie walks in front, white faced and expressionless. I walk two steps behind but I intend to go in with her. I can't let her take all the blame. Some of it was my fault. I try to look brave, but my insides are fluttering like a sparrow in a box.

Outside Sister's office is a waiting area with easy chairs and a coffee table. Neither of us thinks of sitting down. The smart chairs are for the visitors. We stand up straight with our backs to the wall, gazing at the large black crucifix that hangs over Sister's office. The body of Jesus is leaning forward and you can see the agony on his face and the spots of blood around the nails upon his hands and feet. I try to think of the suffering of Jesus and tell myself that nothing Marie and I are about to go through can be nearly as bad as that but, by the time Sister Frances opens the door and calls for Marie to go inside, I'm not feeling quite so sure.

'Did you want something, Teresa?' Sister asks me.

I swallow hard. 'I've come with Marie,' I tell her. 'I've come to give her some moral support.'

Sister Frances looks a bit confused. 'Well, you'd better come inside,' she says.

Inside the office is like a church. It has an altar on a cloth-covered table and pictures of the Blessed Virgin on the walls.

'Blessed Mary, Mother of Jesus,' I mutter under my breath. 'If you get me out of this one, then I promise I'll be good.'

Sister flits across the room with her black habit flapping like a bat in flight. 'Sit down.' She points to two plastic chairs on the other side of her desk. I want to giggle. I don't know why. I think about Marie's story about the girl who laughed and went hysterical when she felt scared and I think I'm a bit like that. I hope I don't show myself up.

Sister sits opposite us. I try not to look at her warts and the long, quivering hairs which sprout from them like floating tentacles. I look at the pictures and writing on the walls:

Teach me, O Lord,
to be patient
and help me to use
every minute in thy service
that of Thy gifts
nothing may be lost or wasted.

'Ms Maltby gave me this.'

At the very name of Ms Maltby I nearly leap out of my seat. My heart starts pounding like a road drill. I grip hold of the underside of the plastic edging on my chair. It doesn't have any arms.

Sister Frances holds up Marie's English book. 'I understand that this was set as an exercise to take all term, but you finished yours within the first two weeks.'

Marie looks down at her feet in shame. 'Yes, Sister.'

Sister opens the book, glancing through the story. 'A most unusual piece of writing.'

She turns the pages over thoughtfully. 'A very mature style of writing for a young woman of your age.'

'Thank you, Sister.'

'And a very well-developed plot.'

Marie just nods.

'What does concern me . . .' Sister glances over the top of the book at this point and looks directly at Marie . . . 'is the ending. The . . .' she searches for the right word . . . 'the *sense of pessimism*. Do you understand what I mean?'

Marie looks thoughtful. 'No, Sister.'

Sister looks across at the Virgin Mary on the wall. 'Most of the great literature of the world . . . most of the *stories* are about the perennial conflict between good and evil.'

Marie and I both nod and try to look intelligent.

'Nearly all of our literature in fact, is about the triumph of the human spirit, about the vitory of good over evil. I think many writers see it as their duty . . . perhaps in thanks to God for their many gifts and talents, they write pieces which will glorify His name.'

I don't really see from this how she's going to get the subject round to us locking Ms Maltby in the stockroom.

'This story . . .' Sister points her immaculate neatly clipped fingernail at the book. '. . . is about the triumph of evil. It's about two girls who are lost and never found. We have the personification of the forces or evil – the vampire . . .'

'They're not real though, Sister,' Marie explains. 'They were only like models, like an effigy.'

'But they do triumph, don't they?' Sister asks her.

Marie doesn't know what to say.

'Don't you think the girls could have been rescued? What about the matron or the mother from the children's home? Surely she wouldn't have slept until the girls were found?'

'But, it was an assessment centre, Sister – not a convent or a school,' says Marie.

'But surely someone, would feel a concern. It's rather like . . . like when you rescued Ms Maltby from the stockroom.'

I feel the blood drain from my face.

'That was a situation of despair. For her it must have seemed like the triumph of the forces of darkness and then . . . then you came. You came along and rescued her.'

The silence hangs between us in the room.

'Didn't you?'

Shame seeps to every corner of my body till I feel like a lump of slime.

'So there we had a story with a . . . with a *happy* ending.'

Nobody says anything.

'Didn't we?'

Marie nods weakly.

'If you hadn't turned up, it would have been like, well, like this story.' Sister gave Marie's book a little pat. 'Despair and pessimism. We rely on people helping each other, taking risks, determination – things that enoble the spirit.'

There's a silence; neither of us knows what to say.

After a few moments, Marie looks up. 'I was thinking of writing it as a play,' she says.

Sister Frances looks interested. 'Mmm?'

'Ms Maltby has been telling us about video and television scripts. About how to write them.' Marie pauses.

Sister nods with encouragement.

'I thought that . . . with the rest of the time – while the others were writing their stories – I could be writing this out as a play. I could write parts for everyone in the class. I thought perhaps Ms Maltby might let us make a video.'

'Mmmmm, well . . .' Sister Frances looks a bit unsure. 'We'll have to ask Ms Maltby what she thinks about that.' She pauses. 'And what about the ending?'

'I suppose I could think about changing it.'

Sister Frances nods. 'I think that would be a good idea.'

Marie and I just don't know what to think.

Breaktime's over now but we don't want to go straight back to Maths. We rush down the corridor and check there's no one looking then sneak into the toilets to collapse.

'Don't you think she knows?' I gasp, as soon as we're inside with the door shut.

'I can't believe it. I just can't believe it.' Marie says, shaking her head.

'She must know.'

'I'm sure she does,' Marie leans against a washbasin. The penalty for sitting on a washbasin is two nights in detention. 'She knows but she hasn't got the evidence.'

'She can't do anything then, can she?'

Marie thinks for a moment. 'She's probably put a curse on us – that's what she's done. She can't do anything *overtly*, so while she was saying – she starts taking off Sister Frances

59

now — *a most unusual piece of writing . . . a very mature style* she was really thinking: *Turn into frogs; turn into frogs; abracadabra, grow webbed feet and warts.*

We both collapse into giggles. Then Marie puts her hands out over me as if she's casting a spell — *'This is a child of Satan,'* she says, *'Her body will turn into a frog and she will be condemned to live in a pond of green slime.'* She takes some of the green liquid soap out of the dispenser on the wall and tries to wipe it on my face. I squeal and run away, then Marie starts chasing me round the toilets.

'Condemned to live upon a lily pad, pondering the conflict between good and evil in the world, pondering, pondering . . .'

The door opens and one of the prefects walks in. We wait for her to go inside one of the toilets and then start giggling again. 'Come on, we'll have to get back.' I pull Marie gently by the arm.

We set off down the corridor towards the Maths room. 'Hey, what's this about a play?' I ask Marie. I ask her very quietly. The penalty for talking in the corridors during lessons is two hundred lines.

'I thought we'd have a trip to Nightmare Park,' she whispers.

'You what?'

'If I write the play, then all our class can go there and make the video.'

'Don't be stupid.' There's no way they'd let us do that. 'We asked if we could go last year . . .'

'Yes, but that was just for a trip.'

'I know, but Sister said we could only go if it was somewhere educational.'

'Yes.' Marie talks to me sometimes as if I'm stupid. 'But this will be educational. We'll be going there to work, won't we?'

I shake my head in disbelief. 'It's no use,' I tell her.

'You'll just waste your time writing it. There's no way, no way, they'd let us go.'

Marie waves her finger at me in another impersonation of Sister Frances. '*Just you wait and see, my girl,*' she tells me. '*Just you wait and see.*'

Nightmare ride at theme park

A secondary school outing turned into a nightmare today when a breakdown occurred on the famous *Satan's Staircase* at Nightmare Park.

The ride takes the form of a giant corkscrew which tunnels underneath an artificial lake by the side of *Dracula's Castle*.

On the last ride of the day, just before closing time, were a party of teenagers from David Blunkett Comprehensive School near Rotherham. Their carriage was halfway through the tunnel when there was a sudden power failure and the teenagers found themselves stranded.

Fifteen-year-old Kelvin Flats from Grimesthorpe was among the party. He said: 'It was terrifying. The walls of the tunnel are painted with ghosts and monsters. It's like a kind of ghost train underground. One or two of us did get out to start walking back but then we were too scared to carry on. We thought we'd sit it out with the others rather than walk back through the tunnel on our own.'

David Sharrow, the park's safety officer, has tried to reassure the public about the park's safety record. At a news conference this evening, he said: 'There was no danger either to these teenagers or to anyone else at the park. Safety checks are carried out every day and there is no possibility of anyone having an accident.'

Nevertheless, it is felt that the incident will have caused some concern to party organizers who have planned visits to the park in the near future.

I cut the article out of the *Daily Sun* and bring it to show Marie. She reads it through at break. 'Mmmmmm,' she says. 'I don't think any of the teachers'll read it, though, do you?'

'I don't know. Why not?'

'Well it isn't the sort of paper they read, is it? You know – nuns and everybody.'

I hadn't thought of that. 'What do they read, then?' I ask her.

'I don't know. I suppose they just read the Bible.'

I'm not so sure about that. 'Are you still writing the play, though?' I ask Marie.

''Course I am. It's going to be really good.' She pats a folder inside her schoolbag. 'I've brought it to show to Mellow Yellow.'

'When? Today?'

Marie nods. She seems to be full of confidence. I still don't think there's any chance that we'll be allowed to actually make the video.

'Don't you remember her saying how she was going to give us something – like a little present?'

'I know, but we can't really expect her to . . .'

'Well, this can be it, can't it? She can take the whole class on a visit to Nightmare Park.'

All the way through English, Marie makes out that she's as good as gold. Ms Maltby walks in wearing a green jumper, brown skirt, beige shoes and she has a brown ribbon in her hair. She looks more or less normal, in fact. To start off with, there's a stunned silence because all the yellow jokes and songs that people have been making up all week just don't apply anymore. Then Roscoe Banks starts singing this song called *I Can Sing a Rainbow*. It goes: *Red and Yellow and Pink and Green, Orange and . . .*'

'Ssshhh!' Marie turns round and hisses at him.

'Terribly sorry,' says Roscoe.

It's a bit later on before he starts singing *Somewhere over the Rainbow*.

Marie turns round again. She speaks quietly but loud enough for Ms Maltby to hear. 'I think that's in very bad taste,' she tells him. 'We had all those silly songs last week.'

He stops singing but a bit later on he starts to hum.

Marie turns round with a look of disgust on her face. 'Don't be so juvenile,' she tells him. 'Remember we've got a *visitor* in school.' She pronounces *visitor* and wags her finger at him the same way that Sister Frances does in Assembly. People smirk and giggle but I don't think Ms Maltby sees the joke.

The lesson is all about scriptwriting. Ms Maltby gives out some copies of plays that have been written as tv scripts and talks about the technical words you use for different camera shots. Marie and I sit listening like angels but everyone else is chattering and messing about.

About halfway through the lesson, a really scruffy-looking man walks in. He has long hair and a bushy beard and he's wearing flared corduroy trousers and a long woolly cardigan that looks like the one our cat sleeps on in her basket. He's carrying a sort of hand-woven sack over his shoulder. He doesn't say anything; he just breezes in and saunters to the back of the classroom. Ms Maltby just ignores him.

After a few minutes, Jez puts his hand up. 'Please, Miss . . .'

'Yes?'

'Please Miss, a tramp's just walked into the classroom.'

People turn round and look at the strange man and giggle. 'He's sitting at the back, Miss.'

Ms Maltby looks a bit pale and weak. She clutches hold of the blackboard rubber for support. 'Class –' she says. 'I'd like to introduce Mr Hoyland. Mr Hoyland is a visitor from the college of education – he's here to supervise students, like myself, who are on their teaching practice.'

Marie and myself turn round and smile politely at Mr Hoyland but the rest of the class just crease up into giggles.

At the end of the lesson, Marie picks up her folder and dashes out to show it to Ms Maltby. She smiles angelically at Mr Hoyland who's just taking out some Rizzlas to roll himself a cigarette. 'I've been writing a video script,' she explains. 'I've based it on the story I wrote – you know the one that you showed Sister Frances?'

Ms Maltby looks a bit harrassed but she smiles at Marie and starts explaining to Mr Hoyland all about the story. I just hover in the background. 'It was extremely well-written,' she tells him. 'Although the ending was rather gruesome.'

Mr Hoyland takes out a tobacco tin with a *Legalise Cannabis* sticker on the lid. I hope he doesn't think he can roll his joints up in our classroom.

'Can I have a look?' He reaches across for the folder.

Marie speaks confidentially to Ms Maltby. 'I'm sorry that some of them haven't been very well-behaved,' she tells her. 'But . . .' she looks at me for moral support, '. . . when the whole class is involved in a project, there's never any trouble at all.'

'Like when we were performing *Godspell*,' I butt in. 'The whole class worked really hard on that.'

Mr Hoyland has been looking through the first few pages of the script which, I notice, Marie has printed immaculately on her father's word processor. 'I looks very impressive,' he says.

He has lots of badges pinned on to his shoulder sack. They say things like: *School Rules – No Way* and *Radical Teachers Say No to Corporal Punishment*. I'm not sure what a radical teacher is but I've a feeling that we might be onto a good thing with Mr Hoyland.

'Would you like a roll-up?' he asks Ms Maltby.

She looks slightly embarrassed. 'Er, no. No thank you.'

I think he's about to offer one to Marie and me as well but then he seems to change his mind.

'I'm not sure whether the school video equipment would be suitable,' Ms Maltby says. 'You've got several indoor scenes with difficult lighting effects and . . .'

'What about the college?' suggests Mr Hoyland. 'The media studies unit's well-equipped. That stuff hardly gets used when the students are out on teaching practice.'

Marie jumps up and down like an excited six-year-old. 'Could we really borrow it?' she asks him. 'That would be really great, wouldn't it?' she kicks me on the ankle.

'Yes. Wonderful.'

'I really believe in giving kids lots of hands-on experience,' he says to Ms Maltby.

I don't know what a *hands-on experience* is but think it means that our class could well be on its way to Nightmare Park.

Everything goes according to plan. Marie persuades Ms Maltby to let her direct the video and she organizes everyone in the class. She makes sure that everybody has a part – even if it's only as an extra – and then lines people up for jobs like costumes and make-up, lighting, continuity and stage manager. The only person who doesn't have a proper job is Ms Maltby but that doesn't really matter; everyone in the class is so well-behaved now that all she has to do is sit and watch.

Marie has explained to everybody that we won't be shooting the video in the same order as the story. In the first part – when the title comes on and before the play properly starts – you'll see all the rides at Nightmare Park. There'll be people screaming as they hurtle down the *Satan's Stairway* and go inside the ghost train – those scenes will be shot last of all when we go on our famous trip. (Marie has smiled sweetly at Mr Hoyland, had long conversations with him about Pink Floyd and Bob Dylan and persuaded him to see Sister Frances and organize the trip for us.)

Then we'll be cutting to the scene where Kimberley gets sent to the assessment centre – it'll be a court scene, like a sort of trial. That doesn't come into Marie's story but we'll be doing it in the video.

The parts that Marie has written for all the class to join in are where Kimberley and Hazel are at the assessment centre. None of us has ever been to one so we don't know what it would be like, but we've heard rumours that they have lots of P.E. and exercise and it's a bit like being in the army.

'Everybody can be doing some kind of drill in the playground,' Marie explains. 'That's just to give an impression of the centre. Then we'll cut to the shots of Hazel and Kimberley in their room afterwards, planning their escape, and then show them climbing out of the window and running away. I thought they could climb out of the library window and clamber down the drainpipe.'

Bernadette Dronfield is playing the part of Kimberley. 'Isn't that a bit dangerous?' she says. 'I don't want to break anything.'

'Yeah. Like the drainpipe,' says Roscoe. Everybody laughs, particularly as Bernadette is somewhat overweight – and that's putting things politely.

Marie has asked the stage manager – that's Tony

Deepcar – to work out a schedule for the rehearsal so everyone knows what they're supposed to do in every lesson. We're not shooting the video straightaway, of course, we're going through all the scenes – rehearsing them and getting everything ready for when Mr Hoyland arrives with all the college equipment.

I've been helping Marie out in the evenings. What she's done is list everybody's job on one of the discs on her father's computer and then, next to all the jobs, she's printed them out a checklist. Like, with the costumes for example, she's listed all the characters that are likely to cause any problems like:

DRACULA

GHOST

FEMALE VAMPIRE

WOLFMAN

She's left spaces next to each one for a list of all their different items of clothing and things like make-up and false teeth. We've decided to leave Frankenstein out of the video because we thought his costume would be a bit too complicated.

Jeremy Rawmarsh – that's Jez – is the property manager, so he has a list that says things like:

SKELETON

COFFINS (2)

CANS OF COKE (3)

BLUE STROBE LIGHT

The blue light is instead of a police car. The idea is that Jez will hide behind a hedge and run up and down with a flashing disco strobe light in his hand and people will think that he's a police car. I'm not sure whether that'll work or not.

The rehearsals take three weeks. We have to get everything done quickly because Ms Maltby's teaching practice only lasts six weeks. Mr Hoyland is coming in the fourth week with all the equipment from the college and he's going to help us shoot the scenes that are set in and around our school. In the last week we're having our longed-for trip to Nightmare Park.

'Are you sure that Sister Frances knows where we're going?' Bernadette asks Marie as we all gather in the hall at break. 'You know, I just can't believe she's given permission for it.'

'She won't understand what it is, though, will she?' says Marie. 'I mean, she won't have seen it advertised on TV or anything.'

Tony laughs. 'What would she say if she knew that we were all going down *Satan's Staircase*?'

All of us start to get excited. 'Hey, is everybody going on that?' asks Jez.

''Course we are,' says Roscoe.

Everyone nods. 'What's it like?' asks Bernadette.

People start explaining all at once.

'It's like a corkscrew ride that goes underground?'

'It goes underneath this lake.'

'It's like a ghost train where you go upside down.'

'Did you read about when those kids got stuck – when their train broke down under the lake?'

'Let's all go on together – all in one big train.'

'Well, what I'm looking forward to,' says Marie, 'is the Gingerbread House.'

69

'What's that?' I ask her.

'Well, first of all there's this lake.' Marie spreads out her hands to demonstrate – as though some of us don't even know what a lake is. 'And the *Gingerbread House* is on an island.'

'And they have ghosts to take you across the lake,' Roscoe interrupts.

'Be quiet,' Marie tells him. 'I'm describing this. Right, you get into a boat and then a ghost rows you across to the island.'

'They're not rowing boats,' Roscoe interrupts. 'They have big sticks – like punts – they're like the ones they have in Italy.'

Neither Roscoe nor Marie has actually been to Nightmare Park. They've just been reading all the brochures about it seventeen hours a day.

'Gondolas,' Marie explains. 'Right so this ghost gondalizes you across the lake and leaves you outside the *Gingerbread House*. And then you get into another boat – this one doesn't have any oars or anything . . .'

'How does it move then?' I ask her.

'There's a water pump,' says Roscoe, 'to move the water along.'

'It's like fishing the ducks at the fair,' Marie explains. 'You know when all the plastic ducks go round in a circle and you have to fish one out?'

I nod.

'And the *Gingerbread House* is all like – as if it's made of icing and sugar – like the one in the fairy story.'

'Hansel and Gretel.'

'That's right. Well, in Hansel and Gretel there was a witch. She made the house like that so she could lure little boys and girls there and then she put them in cages and fattened them up.'

Sister Frances starts to walk across the hall. Everyone

starts to giggle but Marie carries on with the story regardless.

'The only real failing she had was that she couldn't see very well so she didn't know when the children were fat enough to eat. She asked Hansel to put his finger outside . . .'

'Good morning.'

'Good morning, Sister.'

Sister Frances hesitates. 'Aren't you the class that's involved in making the video?'

'That's right, Sister.' Everybody nods and looks enthusiastic.

'And is it coming on all right?'

'Yes, thank you, Sister.'

'Very well, thank you, Sister.'

'Mmmm.' Sister Frances looks around the hall. 'I've had a note from Ms Maltby about taking you out in the school minibus. Is that right?'

'Yes, Sister.'

'That's right, Sister.'

We all nod at her like those dogs that people hang up in their cars.

'The problem is – she hasn't told me exactly where you're going.'

There's a sudden silence round the table.

'I was hoping I might be able to see her this break.'

No one says a word.

'Could anybody explain exactly where you're going?'

I look down at the formica topped table. Roscoe gazes at the menu on the wall. Marie finds some dirt to scrape out from under her fingernail. None of us know what to say.

'Apparently it's about two hours drive away.'

We just stare at her expressionless.

'She said something about a park.'

The silence can't go on. Somebody has to speak. We all

look towards Marie. 'Mmmm.' Marie looks up. 'Yes, well . . . we asked Ms Maltby to . . . er . . . find us somewhere suitable to er . . . shoot the video and she mentioned about a park. I think she's er . . . found a suitable park.' She hesitates. 'I think it was Mr Hoyland's idea.'

I don't know how she dare. I really don't. I look at sister's antennae to see whether they've picked up the vibes of the massive lie. I can tell that they're starting to twitch.

Sister looks confused. 'Well, I'll perhaps see Ms Maltby at lunchtime. She must know where the place is.' She hesitates. 'Never mind then, I'm sure she'll have everything under control.'

Three weeks later, Mr Hoyland arrives wearing a black beret and carrying the college's superduper video camera and all the extras to go with it. But we soon discover that the way he interprets 'kids having lots of hands-on experience' is by not letting any of us go near the equipment and working everything himself. Most of us aren't really bothered, but it's a shame for Roscoe Banks because Marie had written him down as *Chief Camera Person* and there isn't much for him to do now except looking after the empty camera case and holding the actual camera just for a few seconds whenever Mr Hoyland needs both hands free to roll his Rizzlas up.

All of us are in the first scene because it's supposed to be at the assessment centre and we're all outside doing exercises in the yard. Even Ms Maltby is in this scene. We stand in rows wearing shorts and plain white T-shirts and Ms Maltby calls out 'Knees bend . . . arms straight . . . one, two, three, four . . .'. Until all of us are gasping with exhaustion. She walks up and down the rows calling out, 'Come on, there. Harder. Put your backs into it. Stand up straight there. Don't bend your knees!' It nearly kills us off.

At last, Marie shouts, 'O.K. Take a break everybody. Sit down and recover.'

We lie on the ground panting and sweating and wondering whether we'll ever be able to walk again and that's when Mr Hoyland tells us that he's forgotten to switch the microphone on.

We sigh and groan and then stagger to our feet and start to go through the scene again, jumping up and down and

73

jogging on the spot. Mr Hoyland adjusts his beret and then marches backwards down one of the rows with the camera on his shoulder. 'Scene One; Take Two. Action!' he shouts, collapsing into Bernadette as she's bending down to touch her toes.

Mr Hoyland's main concern seems to be to save the camera which I suppose is sensible enough, but the only way he can do this is by hugging Bernie round the bottom and falling over with her so they're nearly on the ground. All of us turn away – partly in embarrassment, partly to camouflage the erupting giggles and partly to check that Sister Frances hasn't ventured out on a litter inspection. She'd have a heart attack if she could see.

At breaktime, Marie is fuming. 'What an idiot!' she exclaims. 'What a fool!' She keeps banging her fist on the side of her head. 'Anybody – anybody could have worked that camera better. He's going to ruin everything!'

'Don't you think it'll be all right now?' I ask her.

'Oh yes,' she says sarcastically. 'All right now. After he's forgotten to switch on the mike, seriously injured the main actress, had a severe attack of camera shake (that was his next problem) and spent half an hour faffing about with his beret.'

'Haven't you seen the schedule?' Marie takes out her computer print-out. 'We've only shot the first session and we're now half a day behind. We've still got to do the scene where they climb out of the window, the police car, and the shoplifting . . .'

'Perhaps he'll improve,' says Bernadette.

Mr Hoyland doesn't exactly improve, but Marie makes sure that the rest of us work extra hard to make up. She calls a meeting at the end of the first day to explain that everything else has to go like clockwork to compensate for the amount of time we're wasting on the fact that he doesn't know the first thing about making a video. (Not that any of us did before this week, but that's neither here nor there.)

Clockwork is hardly the word to describe the rest of the week's events. Tuesday's problem is the tuck shop. We were going to shoot the shoplifting scene in the school tuck shop – what we hadn't realized was that they'd decided to use the Sister Frances anti-litter campaign as a chance to stock-take and paint it. So we troop in there with the camera to find it all covered in wet paint and plaster. That gives Jez all of ten minutes to make the English stock room into a corner shop. He clears the text books off the shelves and scatters a few Mars bars and packets of crisps about but the effect is hardly what we wanted.

Escaping from the library window is another problem. I'm supposed to be playing the part of Hazel. We've practised the escape scene a couple of times and it's not been easy to climb out of the library window but we've managed it OK. The first part is very easy. We pretend to wake up in bed at night (We're really lying on two of the library shelves hidden by some sheets – they're supposed to look like bunks) and then we creep over to the window, open it and climb out. What you can't tell on the video – we hope – is that just outside the window is a little balcony so we just walk on there and hide around the corner.

'Sorry,' says Mr Hoyland, 'I've set the camera on *Pause* instead of *Record*. We'll have to tape all that again.'

Meanwhile, unbeknown to us, someone has walked inside the library, noticed the draught from the window and fastened it up. When we turn to go back inside, the window's locked and fastened and there we are – locked out on the balcony in our stripy nightshirts. We both feel really stupid.

We sit, dangling our legs over the edge of the balcony, whilst Mr Hoyland sends someone inside to see about the

75

window. It's just then that we see Sister Frances pacing towards us from her office. We can't do anything about it. We can't get down and it isn't our fault we're stranded so we just sit there watching her.

'Scene six; take three. Action!'

When the window's open we climb through again and throw down these carrier bags that are supposed to contain our clothes. Bernie gets a bit over-enthusiastic and throws hers so far that it hits Mr Hoyland right on the toggle of his beret. He staggers backwards swearing.

What Mr Hoyland doesn't realize is that Sister has just marched into earshot, antannae bristling, and the words he uses are so rude that classes all over school are interrupted as nuns cover up their eardrums and run to shut their classroom windows.

Sister turns pale and looks weak with shock but she staggers first towards Bernadette and myself. 'Girls!' she calls. 'You are exposing yourselves.'

We don't know what to say to that. I think what she means is that our nightshirts only come down to our knees and we're not wearing very much underneath.

'Go inside and get dressed right away,' she orders us.

As we turn to climb back in through the window, we hear her starting on Mr Hoyland. 'Perhaps you'd be kind enough to come down to my office, sir,' she says. We turn and see him picking up his beret and trotting after her down the path.

*

'All we've got on the video so far,' Marie says at the planning meeting, pulling at her hair as if she's about to tear it out, 'is a college lecturer indecently assaulting one of our pupils, two strange figures creeping about the library and some extremely disgusting language.'

76

'Perhaps we should change the story,' says Bernadette. 'We could call it *Corruption in a Catholic School*.'

Marie flashes her a look of total disgust. 'The most important thing we have to do, however, is to organize the trip to Nightmare Park.'

An immediate cheer goes up, interspersed with chanting: *Nightmare Park . . . Nightmare Park . . . Nightmare Park . . .*'

'It seems to me,' says Marie, 'that the main thing is to make sure we get the video out of the way as soon as possible. Then we can spend the rest of the day going on the rides.'

Everyone nods with approval.

'Are we all going to turn up wearing the costumes?' asks Tony. 'Or shall we get changed after we arrive?'

There's a lot of argument, especially from those people who live a long way off. 'I don't want to walk down the street dressed as a vampire,' says Abbi. 'I shall feel like a real nerk.'

'Well, I'm coming as Wolfman,' says Roscoe.

'Well, it doesn't make any difference to you. You look abnormal anyway.'

Tony Deepcar is the stage manager and he's supposed to be in charge of things like that. 'Look,' he says, 'I think that even if it means coming to school early to get changed, everyone ought to have all their clothes and make-up on ready so we can shoot the video as soon as we arrive.'

'Then I'm off into *Dracula's Castle*,' says Roscoe.

'I thought we were all going on *Satan's Staircase* first,' says Jez. 'We're all going on together.'

Once everybody starts talking about the rides, there's no point in Marie trying to discuss the video. It doesn't matter anyway. All we wanted out of the whole performance was a day out in Nightmare Park. None of us can wait for Friday morning.

77

Schoolchildren disappear in Nightmare Park

Police are investigating the mysterious disappearance of two teenagers, Ann Stone and Norton Woodseats who were last seen on Friday evening at Nightmare Park amusement centre.

The two teenage sweethearts, both fourth formers from the Edith Hattersley Comprehensive School near Doncaster were last seen by their fellow pupils walking hand in hand by the edge of Nightmare Park's artificial lake. Both were wearing faded blue denim jeans and training shoes.

Their teacher, Mrs Elsie Carr from Swallownest said last night that the young couple seemed perfectly happy and she could think of no reasons whatsoever for their sudden disappearance.

'The pupils were all very well-behaved,' she told our reporter. 'There was no horseplay or messing about and I really don't see how any of them could have had an accident.'

Nightmare Park's safety officer, Mr David Sharrow has arranged for a team of frogmen to search the artificial lake which was also the scene of the disappearance last year of a young trainee, Wayne Gate.

Police are continuing their investigations.

NIGHTMARE PARK

A JOURNEY
INTO *FEAR*

Sister Frances
Notre Dame High School
Malin Bridge.

Dear Sister Frances

Thank you for your letter. I am very pleased to hear about your school's proposed visit to Nightmare Park and am happy to reassure you that you need have no concern at all for the safety of your pupils.

Safety checks are carried out daily on all the major rides at the park and, in fact, in spite of recent publicity, we have the best safety record to date of any such large amusement centre.

The cases you mentioned involved young people who have been reported missing. As I'm sure you are aware, many thousands of young people disappear from their homes each year. In each case, there is a location where they have last been sighted – often a bus station, public house or café. On two occasions, teenagers who have been reported missing have been last sighted at Nightmare Park. After carrying out the most extensive investigations, we are convinced that these young people have come to no harm at the park. The evidence suggests that they have decided to leave home for some reason and have used the crowded anonymity of the park to conceal their departure.

I hope you will find this letter gives you the reassurance you need and I wish your pupils a happy and enjoyable day with us.

Yours sincerely

David Sharrow

Mr. D. Sharrow, M.Sc., FRICS

'Did you see it on Friday about Nightmare Park?' asks Abbi.

Everybody seems to have seen or heard something over the week-end about the missing teenagers. 'Do you think it'll stop us going?' asks Jez.

The door opens and Sister Frances strides into the classroom. 'Oh no, now for it,' groans Marie.

We scutter to our places and sit down.

Sister produces a folder full of letters. 'These are for your parents,' she explains, 'to tell them all the arrangements for your visit – what time they can expect you home, what you're going to do about lunch and so forth.' She looks round the class to make sure that everyone is paying attention. 'Now, I do know that some of your parents may be extremely worried if they've read certain recent items in the newpapers, so I'm also enclosing with each letter a copy of the communication I've received from the park's safety officer.'

'Now who's going to give these out for me?'

Several people volunteer. Sister gives the letters to Roscoe and Abbi. 'Now,' she says, 'there is nothing more important for us here at Notre Dame than your welfare and safety – you know that don't you?'

We nod obediently.

'So you can tell your parents that all precautions are being taken and you'll be properly supervized all the time you're at the park.'

'She'll probably send us all in leg irons,' Marie groans as soon as Sister's gone.

'We'll probably have to walk in in twos,' Jez suggests, 'like we used to do in the Infants.'

'Or in a crocodile,' I suggest.

'All chained together in a big long row.'

'We'll probably have to have little name badges on,' says Abbi, 'in case we get lost.'

Most of us laugh but Marie just sits and shakes her head. 'Nothing is going to stop us now,' she says. 'Nothing.' She raises the letter from Sister Frances high up into the air. 'Nightmare Park,' she shouts. 'Here we come.'

Everybody cheers.

We look a real sight waiting for the mini bus. There are two coffins over by the wall and standing next to them are Wolfman, Dracula and one of the ghosts. The ghost is carrying a rucksack over his shoulder with his sandwiches in and a flask. Then there's Abbi Dale, the female vampire with a deathly white face, stacks of black eye-liner, and wearing a black bomber jacket under which is an ankle-length white nightdress. Jez is running up and down by the side of the hedge with his blue strobe light making a noise like a police siren and next to him is Ms Maltby with two first aid boxes, an ordnance survey map and a register to check that we're all here.

The last person to arrive is Mr Hoyland. Everyone cheers when his Citroen 2CV comes chugging around the corner in a cloud of blue smoke. We all pile across to help him unload the camera and stuff. 'Can you just help me carry these out of the car?' he says to Jez.

'Car?' says Tony, behind his back. 'I thought it was a pram with a motor inside.'

'I think you need a new exhaust pipe, sir,' suggests Abbi.

'I bet the car's taking after him and started chain smoking,' says Bernie.

Mr Hoyland staggers out of the car with the camera and boxes of equipment. He's wearing a *Free Nelson Mandella* T-shirt and a *Save the Whale* badge on his beret. 'Hi there!' he shouts at Ms Maltby, waving his shoulder sack at her.

Ms Maltby looks slightly embarrassed as she gives him a little wave.

Mr Hoyland walks across and nearly sits on one of the

coffins. Tony stops him just in time. 'You'd better not sit there,' he tells him. 'They're only made of cardboard.'

'Oh sorry. Can you hold this lot then?' He passes some of the equipment to Tony. 'I'll have to get a roll-up before we start.'

Just then a massive cheer erupts as the mini bus emerges round the corner. Everybody clusters to the front, '*Nightmare Park . . . Nightmare Park . . .*' The chanting starts as people gather up their gear and surge forward.

'Come on,' says Ms Maltby. 'Be sensible now. Form a queue.'

There's no holding everybody back – the excitement is so infectious.

'*Nightmare Park . . . Nightmare Park.*'

'Come on, now. There'll be enough seats for everybody.'

The first awareness that I have that anything is wrong is when I see the expression on Tony Deepcar's face. He's standing at the edge of the road, looking really excited, still holding on to all Mr Hoyland's stuff when suddenly, his face just seems to collapse. His whole body sags as he stares in amazement at the mini bus. Then the chanting starts to trail off. People are standing open-mouthed and staring. I have a horrible premonition of disaster. Something is drastically wrong. I turn and look in the direction of the bus.

Oh no. I blink. A wave of shock is carried through the crowd. I blink again. I just can't believe my eyes; but as the mini bus pulls up at the side of the road, there's no escaping from the truth.

There, sitting in the front, resplendent in her black habit and matching anorak is Sister Frances. Sister Frances is the one who's driving us to Nightmare Park.

We file on to the bus in stunned, shocked silence, filling it from the back. Nobody wants to sit anywhere near the front. The last two seats have to be taken by Mr Hoyland and Ms Maltby. Sister turns and gazes without expression at the cardboard coffins, the Dracula suit, the mad monk and even Wolfman. At the sight of Mr Hoyland's lighted cigarette, however, her eyes blaze down like exocet missiles and the notorious black antennae start quivering like arrows in a target.

Mr Hoyland wilts like a dehydrated daffodil then stubs his cigarette between his fingers and throws it out the door.

Sister starts the engine.

At first there's silence as the awful truth is registered: Sister Frances really is coming with us to Nightmare Park.

'It's his fault,' Marie mutters under her breath.

'What do you mean?'

'She doesn't trust him with us.'

I'm not sure what she means by that. 'Why doesn't she?'

Marie grins. 'She thinks he'll be teaching us to smoke and swear. Telling us who Nelson Mandella is. She thinks he might corrupt us.'

I grin.

As we set off, the first thing I notice is the speed at which Sister drives the bus. I would have expected her to drive slowly and sedately – the way she normally moves around – but instead, she pulls out straight into the fast lane and stays there, rattling along at full power, refusing to let anyone overtake, I hang on to the window catch.

I would never have thought that a bus full of schoolkids could be so quiet. The only sounds apart from the engine are the scraping of Sister's gears and the honking of irate drivers.

'We'll get away from her, won't we?' I say to Marie.

She nods her head. 'The sooner the better.' She clings hold tightly to the folder in which she's collected all her copies of the scripts. 'We'll have to formulate a plan.'

Both of us are suddenly thrown against the window as the minibus screeches round a corner. On our right we can see the driver of the sports car that Sister has just overtaken on the inside lane. He raises his fingers as if he's about to make a rather rude sign but, when he sees a nun driving the bus, he crosses himself instead.

Sister gives him a regal wave and rattles on regardless.

'We'll have to arrange a rendezvous,' Marie says.

'What's that?'

'Like a secret meeting place.' Marie gets thrown against me again as we swing round another corner. 'When we've finished the video, we'll all sneak off – she'll never be able to find us – it'll be much too crowded – and then we'll all meet up, say at *Satan's Staircase* at 12 o'clock.'

'We'll have to tell everybody then.'

Marie starts to get out of her seat then looks forward at Sister Frances. 'Perhaps I'd better pass a note round,' she decides.

As Marie takes out her pen and paper, I look out of the window and realize that we're joining the motorway. I start to feel slightly worried. 'Do you think she's passed her driving test?' I ask Marie.

'Course she has. She must have.'

The traffic slows into single file as we approach some road works. The inside lane, which is being dug up, is cordoned off with cones. Sister revs the engine with impatience as the traffic slows to a halt.

'Do you think 12 o'clock's too early?'

I look at my watch. 'Better make it one.'

'OK.'

The traffic idles forward. Sister keeps pulling out but there's no possibility that we can overtake. Suddenly, we're thrown back against our seats as she glimpses a larger-than-average gap between the cones over on our left. She veers the bus round in between the cones and careers down the blocked-off lane towards the road works. My heart turns over as I see the yawning hole ahead of us. 'Oh no,' I put my hand up to my mouth. Just before we're about to plummet down the massive hole, Sister slaloms back into the mainstream of traffic, sandwiching our bus between a frozen-food lorry and a cattle truck. A dozen or more drivers peep their horns at us, but the only response is a loud and prolonged mooing from the cattle truck. Sister sits inscrutable.

We lean back sighing with relief. 'We needn't bother going to Nightmare Park,' I hear Roscoe muttering from behind. 'It's more scary sitting here with Batwoman driving than it'll be on *Satan's Stairway*.'

Ms Maltby had told us that the journey would take about two hours; with Sister Frances at the wheel it takes just over fifty five minutes.

We can hardly believe it when we see the gates of Nightmare Park looming up before us. 'We're here. Look.' I nudge Marie in excitement. 'Look out the window. We're nearly there.'

The word gets passed along the bus. If Sister wasn't with us, we'd have cheered; as it is, people are bobbing up and down and pointing and starting to get excited but everything's held in check. No one dares to start chanting or shouting or even look too enthusiastic.

Sister completely ignores the attendant who's pointing out a space in the row of cars right at the bottom of the car park; instead she zigzags round him and screeches the bus to a halt right next to the main gate just in front of a sign that says *OFFICIALS ONLY*.

We're thrown backwards with the shock as she heaves on the handbrake and switches off the engine. 'Right,' she stands up and turns around to face us. 'I shall be leaving the mini bus unlocked at the back, so you must take all your valuables with you. 'Now . . .' she scowls up and down the rows . . . 'you must all be particularly careful not to go near

86

the water. There have been several accidents to young people at this park and I don't want your names adding to the list.'

'So much for the scene where we balance on the log flume,' I mutter to Marie.

'It doesn't matter. We'll do it when she's not looking.'

'As a precaution, I have brought one or two items of spare clothing.' Sister holds up a carrier bag which, instead of being inscribed with the usual *Sainsbury's* or *Chelsea Girl*, has a crucifix on the front and the words, *Blessed are the Meek for they shall inherit the Earth*.

'There are a couple of track suits in here – just in case anything should happen to any of you, and . . .' She holds up another bag with *Blessed are the Merciful, for they shall obtain Mercy* on it . . . 'in here are some first aid boxes. If you should fall down or hurt yourselves,' she explains, 'you can come back here and take a plaster or whatever.'

'Good grief! It's just like being in the Reception class,' Marie mutters through clenched teeth.

'Last of all, having looked at the illustrations on some of the brochures I thought it might be a good idea to bring each of you one of these.'

'Oh no,' says Marie, 'I just can't believe it.'

From a carrier inscribed, *Blessed are the Pure in Heart, for they shall see God*, she takes a bundle of plastic bags.

'Sick bags!' All of us are nearly collapsing in hysterics.

Sister waves her antennae at us and we try to compose ourselves.

'Now take all your belongings with you, and line up in twos over by the gate.'

Nightmare Park is even more exciting than we expected. As soon as we file in through the huge portcullis gates we're surrounded by an ocean of sight and sound. There are vampires wailing, chains clanking, ghost trains rattling and people screaming from every corner. Cable cars glide over our heads, we can feel vibrations under our feet and the air is perfumed with a beautiful mixture of hot dogs, chips, toffee apples, bhajis and curry sauce. I can hardly wait to explore.

'Let's hurry up and finish the video,' Roscoe mutters. 'We want to go on all the rides.'

'What shall we shoot first?' asks Mr Hoyland.

'Well, we could start with Sister Frances,' Marie giggles.

'We'd better do the parts where we're in costume first,' she says out loud. 'Then people can take their clothes and props back to the bus.' She bends down and whispers in my ear, 'We can disappear then. Let him do all the shots of the rides and everything.'

I nod. It sounds like a good idea.

Marie opens her brochure at the map on the first page. 'We need to find *Dracula's Castle*,' she explains. 'That's where we're going to shoot the parts with Kimberley and Hazel.'

We turn and look around. Towering over the bottom end of the park is a huge black gothic castle. 'There it is. Look,' Mr Hoyland points out. 'Come on.'

We start to thread our way through the park. Funnily enough, those in costume don't look out of place at all. They just blend in with the scenery. We try to take in all the rides and sounds and smells without getting too distracted. Near the gate are rows of stalls selling food and souvenirs. There are black rubber bats dangling on elastic, plastic masks and totem poles. Other stalls sell badges, stickers, mugs and T-shirts saying, *Nightmare Park – A Journey into Fear* and *I Rode the Nightmare and Survived*.

'Look at the cable cars!' says Abbi. As we get nearer to the mountain, we can see people riding on cable cars which seem to be coming out of the back of the castle.

'And look at that drop!' says Bernadette. Plunging down the front of the mountain is an almost vertical slide. Tiny figures, with their arms stretched into the air, seem to leap off the edge of the mountain and disappear from view. Above their heads stands a huge notice saying:
Death Drop.

The most exciting thing we pass – or that passes us, rather – is just above our heads. We're so busy looking at the different stalls and the mountain looming up before us that none of us notice a track, like a big dipper, stretching above the path. Not until the train comes past. There's an oncoming sound like a roll of thunder, then the wailing of a siren from the sky. As we look up, we see a train load of screaming figures hurtling above the Batbar Takeaway, careering upside down into a corkscrew, screeching across the path in front of us and then, apparently, disappearing into a hole inside the ground. All of us rush forward to try and see where they've gone.

'Wow! Did you see that?'

'It's the *Satan's Staircase*!'

'That's where they go underground'

As I dash around the corner, I can hardly believe my eyes. The ground dips away below us into a large valley. Around the edges of the valley is a forest of pine trees and, in the middle, is what appears to be an enormous eyeball.

'What's that?'

'I don't know.'

'It looks like a lake.'

'It can't be.'

'It is. Look, there're boats sailing on it.'

Marie opens out her map. 'Look. Here!' she exclaims. 'This is it. It's called the *Evil Eye*.'

'What is it?'

'It's a lake.'

'No, it isn't. It can't be.'

'It is, look. It's got boats on it.'

I look more closely and realize that it's true. Strange shrouded figures are steering boats full of people across the surface of the eyeball.

'Look, there!' Marie actually starts jumping up and down. 'Look. There in the middle.'

'What is it?'

Marie points her brochure towards the centre of the eyeball. Her face lights up with excitement. 'It's the *Gingerbread House*!'

It's hard to see it at first because you have to look in between the pine trees, but it's true. The eyeball really is a lake and in the middle is an island. That's where the ghosts are rowing people on the boats. In the centre of the island is what looks like a fairy-tale cottage. It has a thatched, barley-sugar roof and windows that seem to be made of sugar icing. Marie is right: it's the *Gingerbread House*.

'Oh, I've got to take a picture.' Marie puts everything down and starts to take out her brand new camera. So does virtually everyone else who's brought a camera with them. I'm about to tell them that they can take their pictures later, that we want to get on with the video, but I don't want to spoil their fun. I wait patiently, holding people's coats and bags.

'Look. There's the Corkscrew!'

I look across and see the train emerging from the lake.

Then it spirals inside the pine forest and disappears from view.

'There's another one coming!'

This time we can follow where it goes. We hear the siren and the screams. We hear the thunder overhead. We see the rows of terror-stricken faces as they caterpillar overhead and then we see the Corkscrew plummeting downwards as it drills inside the ground.

'That's where it goes under the lake.'

It vanishes. We feel a vibration underneath our feet but there's nothing else to show the passage of the Corkscrew. The trees are still, the water is smooth on the lake; there's no clue whatsoever where it's gone.

'Where's it go to then?'

'Underneath the lake. It's like a ghost train.'

'Where does it come out?'

'Over there.' Marie points. 'Oh, I want a photo of it.'

A dozen different cameras are trained on the spot where the Corkscrew comes back into view. 'There it is. Look!' I can't help being carried along with the excitement, even though I don't even own a camera.

The cameras click and Tony starts to get impatient. 'Come on,' he says. 'We all want to go on it; the queues'll be massive later on.'

Marie can hardly tear herself away. 'Oh I really want to go inside the *Gingerbread House*,' she tells everyone.

'There'll be plenty of time,' says Jez. 'Come on, let's get up to the castle.'

Sister Frances walks besides us, saying nothing. I don't know what she thinks about it all. Mr Hoyland walks at the back with Ms Maltby. He seems to be trying to explain to her about how to make a video but Ms Maltby doesn't look impressed.

We walk along the path that goes around the edge of the

forest underneath the cable cars. At the foot of the *Magic Mountain*, as it's called, there's a crossroads. You can either go on the path that takes you right inside the mountain – that has a notice saying *See the Evil Goblins try to steal the Dwarfs Treasure* – we decide that's really just for little kiddies; or you can go on the *Iron Maiden* which takes you up to the castle.

The *Iron Maiden* is a lift which looks like an instrument of medieval torture. It's a kind of bottomless cage that opens outwards and you stand inside with your feet on some iron bars. Sister Frances takes one look at it and shakes her head. So does Ms Maltby.

'I don't think it'll be as painful as it looks,' says Mr Hoyland helpfully.

'Don't they have any steps?' asks Ms Maltby.

Marie consults the map. 'There are some steps round the other side,' she points out.

Sister looks down at the carboard coffins that Tony and Jez are carrying. 'Well, you won't be able to take those up on the lift will you?' she says curtly.

'We can carry them for you,' Ms Maltby offers. 'They don't look very heavy.'

Sister looks a bit reluctant but she accepts the coffin that Tony passes to her. 'We'll set off and find the steps then,' she tells us. 'Mr Hoyland can look after you and we'll meet you at the top.'

Marie grins mischievously as Sister disappears round the corner with the coffin underneath her arm. '. . . in about two hours time,' she says. 'It says here: *Please Note – There are over two hundred steep steps to the top of the Magic Mountain. This route is not recommended for the elderly or infirm.*'

The cages are joined together by a clanking chain. When my turn comes I have to place my feet inside two things like

92

iron stirrups. It seems very scary to be carried upright with my back to the mountainside but there are some supports underneath my armpits and two iron circles to hold on to. The other half of the cage is clamped across me and, as the huge chain starts to lift my cage up the mountain side, I keep telling myself that there's no way I can fall out.

I grin down at Abbi who's just climbing inside her cage and I try to look up at Tony and Jez who've gone in front but I can't see upwards. I can't even see their feet. I stare out straight ahead and, as the cage ascends, I have a panoramic view of Nightmare Park. It's lovely. I can see over the tops of the trees and I can see the *Satan's Staircase* with the Corkscrew hurtling along its track. I'm all right until the cage gives a little jerk and I look down and see the lake and start to think about the newspaper cutting Marie showed me about the boy who they say fell from *Dracula's Castle* and was never seen again. Then I close my eyes.

*

Mr Hoyland has to walk up the steps as well.

'He couldn't get his camera inside the *Iron Maiden*,' Tony explains.

'Well, there was no need for him to use such disgusting language,' says Marie. 'Sister Frances could have been corrupted.'

I can't honestly see the chance of anyone being able to corrupt Sister Frances but I don't say anything.

We wait for the others to come up on the *Iron Maiden* then we walk over to the castle. It looks great. It's really huge and menacing with bats flying up around the towers. I suppose they must be mechanical but they look very realistic. Every now and then, a figure of a ghost or a vampire appears on top of the battlements or at one of the high slit windows. They look really spooky. Around the castle is a circular moat with a heavy chained drawbridge across. People are rowing on boats around the moat and underneath the drawbridge.

'Shall we go in the castle?' says Roscoe. 'We can be out before they've finished climbing all the steps.'

'No,' says Marie. 'We'd better work the video out first.'

'We could just go on a rowing boat.'

Marie ignores him. 'If we put the coffins in a dark corner with the black wall behind, then it might look as though they're really inside the castle.'

Roscoe looks wistfully at the rowing boats. 'I know what we could do,' he says. 'For that bit where everybody has to glide past we could pull one of the boats up to the edge here.' He points down into the water. 'Dracula or whoever could stand up in it and we could push it along. I mean, you wouldn't see the boat or their feet or anything.'

Marie frowns. 'I don't know. We were going to stand on the log flume to do that.'

'But that'll be right out in the open where it's light,' Roscoe complains. 'It's really dark here with all the towers and everything.'

'Mmmm. Well, perhaps we could give it a try.'

Abbi and Roscoe sprint to the queue to get a rowing boat. People give them some funny looks. It isn't so bad seeing strange monsters walking around the park because everything here is weird, but people look a bit uneasy when they realize that both Wolfman and a vampire are standing next to them in the queue for the rowing boats.

Marie rushes to explain the new arrangements to Mr Hoyland when he comes puffing up the steps.

Mr Hoyland doesn't look enthusiastic. He spends a long time struggling to get his breath then collapses on the battlements and takes out his tobacco tin. Marie glowers over him as he unfolds his packet of Rizzlas.

Then Sister Frances arrives, panting and red-faced, with

94

her coffin under her arm. Her black woolly stockings are wrinkled round her ankles and her habit is covered with an assortment of leaves and branches. She looks as though she's tried to take a short cut through the forest. And she doesn't look very pleased.

Sister turns and waits for Ms Maltby who seems in an even worse state. Her coffin seems to be on the verge of collapse. In fact, half of it has unravelled, exposing the baked bean cartons and sellotape which should be hidden underneath the teak wallpaper. 'I'm terribly sorry,' she explains. 'I got the corners tangled in a tree.'

Marie sighs. 'Never mind, it'll have to do.'

She turns around to Jez. 'Right, can you put the coffins over in that corner?'

Jez picks up the coffins and we start to get organized. 'Now,' says Marie, 'Terri and Bernie – if you can look as though you're sitting on the coffins but really – if you could just crouch down so you're not putting any weight on them.' She turns to Mr Hoyland. 'That'll be a medium 2-shot,' she explains.

Mr Hoyland gets the camera together whilst Bernie and I crouch down over the coffin.

'Action!'

We open the can of Coke and sit there drinking.

'Sorry,' says Mr Hoyland, 'I shot into the light there. Can we take that one again?'

We start again with another can of Coke only to have a troop of Girl Guides walk straight into the shot.

'Cut!' Marie shouts. 'Let's try again. Take three.'

We start to shoot once more just as one of the Girl Guides walks up behind Sister Frances and reaches out to touch her. She obviously thinks that Sister's an exhibit – like one of the vampires on the tower. When Sister turns round and glares at her the poor girl nearly collapses in hysterics.

Then Bernadette gets the giggles. 'Shhh,' I tell her. 'Compose yourself.'

'Take Five.'

The camera starts and we're just beginning to drink our Coke again when, Roscoe floats past on his boat. He's wearing his Wolfman outfit and balancing with his arms stretched out like a hairy ballerina. We spurt Coke all over the coffin and fold up especially when he backs into the drawbridge and nearly falls into the water.

'Cut.'

'I'm ever so sorry,' giggles Bernie, 'but – did you see him?' She starts to crease up over again.

Marie sighs heavily. 'All right, just have a break,' she says.

'At last,' says Bernie. 'I can't crouch down here any longer.' And she collapses with all her weight upon the cardboard coffin. I close my eyes. I can hardly bear to look. I open them to find that Bernadette is sprawled out on the floor and the coffin's been flattened into a cardboard pancake. 'When Marie said *Have a Break*,' I chuckle, 'I don't think that's quite what she meant.'

There doesn't seem any possibility of turning the video into a success although, in a way, it doesn't matter, because all we really wanted was to come to Nightmare Park. We shoot the scenes with people floating past in boats but none of them look right because the ghosts and vampires are all rocking backwards and forwards, trying to keep their balance. We also can't stop people walking into the shots. Some kids from other schools even keep jumping right in front of the camera and waving as if they think they're on television.

Marie sits down on the battlements, pulling on her hair. I feel sorry for her because I know she's spent so much time writing out the script and everything, but there's nothing I can do. Sister Frances looks at Marie as if she's about to go across and say something, but then she seems to change her mind.

In the end, Marie walks over to Mr Hoyland. 'Look,' she tells him, 'I think I'm just going to have to abandon this section.'

Mr Hoyland nods in sympathy.

'I think the best thing we can do is get the shots of all the rides and everything. I mean, if you don't mind doing that . . .' she gives him one of her famous winning smiles '. . . you'd be better really without all the distractions, wouldn't you?' She says *distractions* looking at us as if we're a load of performing seals.

Mr Hoyland looks delighted to be able to make the video by himself. I think he's fed up with the way Marie keeps bossing him about.

'Well. OK, then,' he says. 'If you're sure you don't mind.'

'I think it'll be for the best,' she says. 'We'll just have to keep ourselves occupied for the rest of the afternoon.'

We say goodbye to Sister Frances and rush over to the cable cars. We just want to get away. 'I'll see you all back at the bus at six o'clock,' Sister calls out after us.

'Right, Sister.'

'Bye, Sister.'

'Have a good time, Sister.'

It looks a lot more fun to go down the mountain on the *Death Drop*, but the cable cars will give us a really good view of the park and they'll also take us back towards the mini bus. We want to dump the coffins and other props and change into our normal clothes.

Once we're round the corner out of sight we start to skip and dance about. 'Whooo! Freedom!' yells Abbi, jumping on and off the battlements.

'Here we go! Here we go! Here we go!' sings Roscoe.

People turn and stare at the strange assortment of who-oping ghosts and vampires, but we don't care what they think.

First of all, we go on the cable cars. We sit on little seats, two in each car, and ride high above *Death Drop* and the *Enchanted Forest*.

'I wonder what really happened to that boy,' says Marie as our car swings over towards the *Satan's Staircase*.

'Which boy?'

'The one who disappeared from *Dracula's Castle*. I mean, I wonder if they ever found his body.'

'Well, it's not a very good time to talk about it, is it?' I tell her. 'Not when we're up here.'

'Well, he was wearing a football scarf – a Sheffield United

scarf – that's red and white. So, if you see a red and white scarf anywhere, hanging from a tree – or from a cable car . . .'

'Shuttup.'

We pass over the *Satan's Staircase* as the Corkscrew is just about to leave. 'Look,' I point it out to Marie. 'That's where we get on.'

'Right. One o'clock. We should have plenty of time.'

*

Marie and I are first off the cable cars and it doesn't take us long to call back and leave my jacket and Marie's clipboard and folder in the bus.

'We've just got time to walk round the lake,' Marie says, 'before we meet the others. We can see what the queues are like then for the *Gingerbread House*.'

'OK.'

'I can take some more photos as well.'

Marie takes out her map. 'Look, if we go in this other entrance on the right, it comes out by the *Enchanted Forest*.'

'OK.'

We walk through the car park and show our tickets to get back in. Then we go along a narrow path with high hedges on either side that brings us straight out by the lake.

'Oh, just look at the view,' cries Marie. 'Let's take a photograph. Come on, stand over by the water.'

I always feel shy about having my photograph taken. I never know how to stand or how to look. 'Do I have to?'

'Of course you do. Come on.'

I stand at the side of the lake and try to pose.

'Come on, Say Cheese.'

I pull a really mournful face. 'Gorgonzola.'

'Oh brilliant.' Marie lowers the camera.

'Come on, you'll have to let me take one of you now.'

As I'm waiting for Marie to compose herself, I stand and gaze around. There aren't any rides on this side of the lake, so everything is peaceful and quiet. There are trees and bushes and birds singing and I can see the ghosts taking people across the lake to the *Gingerbread House* on the island.

'Is this OK?' Marie is sitting on the edge of a small rock that overhangs the lake.

I crouch down so I'm on the same level as her. Otherwise, I think the picture will come out crooked. There's a ghost floating past.

'I'll see if I can get the ghost in the background as well.'

I lie on my tummy with the camera resting on a rock in front of me. Ms Maltby has told us that's how to avoid the camera shake that Mr Hoyland suffers from.

'Come on then, smile.'

Marie starts to pull a funny face but then something really odd happens. Just when I'm taking the photograph, an old lady rushes up behind Marie. It happens so quickly that I don't really see her. I take the photograph, realize that it's spoilt, then look up and see this woman trying to push Marie into the lake. I can hardly believe it. Marie topples forward and seems just about to lose her balance. Her foot slips over the edge into the water but she manages to keep hold of the rock.

'Look out!' I hear myself shouting.

The old lady looks up and seems really surprised to see me. I must have been hidden from her by the rock. She stands and opens her mouth as if she's about to say something, but then she just hurries off.

I stare after her in amazement.

'Give us a hand.'

I hold out my hand to Marie who's trying to clamber back up the rock. 'Are you OK?'

100

'Yes, I'm all right,' says Marie. 'That woman just bumped into me.'

'I know.' I'm still staring after her incredulously. 'She did in on purpose.'

'Are you sure?'

'Positive.'

We both stare in amazement at where the old lady has just disappeared behind the bushes. 'Did you see her?' Marie asks me.

'Not for long.' I try to remember what she looked like. 'She was quite old with grey hair.'

'Where did she come from?'

'I don't know.' I look around. 'She just seemed to come out from behind the bushes.'

'She must be mad.'

We both just stand and stare. It seems such a ridiculous thing to happen. 'Is she still there?' I ask Marie.

'I don't know.' She creeps over to the bush.

'Be careful.'

I follow her, but there's no one there. The only thing you can see behind the bush is a small jetty and a kind of trap door that looks as though it has something to do with the water in the lake.

Marie stands and looks around. 'Are you sure she was trying to push me in?' she asks, still incredulous. 'I mean, don't you think it must have been an accident . . . ?'

I shake my head. 'It didn't look like it.'

Marie shakes her head in disbelief.

'We'll see when you develop the photos anyway,' I tell her. 'I managed to take her photograph.'

We tell the others about it as we stand in the queue for the *Satan's Stairway*.

'Oh, it must have been an accident,' says Bernadette.

'Perhaps she was really short sighted,' Abbi suggests. 'Perhaps she couldn't see what she was doing.'

'It wasn't like that,' I tell them. 'Honestly. I mean, I'm sure it was on purpose.'

'Perhaps she's just escaped from a mental hospital,' says Roscoe.

'Well, what's she doing here then?' I ask him.

'They might have come on a day trip,' says Jez.'They might have brought all the patients for a day out.'

'That's right,' says Roscoe. 'And they might have all escaped. The whole place'll be full of loonies.'

A crowd of people are just getting off the Corkscrew. They look white-faced and nauseous as they clamber out of the train and begin to stagger away.

I start feeling worried. I'm still quite upset about the old woman and Marie. I keep going over it in my mind, trying to understand what happened.

The queue is very long and, the longer we have to wait, the more scary it seems to get. We can hear the screams of people when they reach the top of the track and look down the first drop.

'Do you remember when those kids went on and the Corkscrew broke down?' says Marie.

That's the last thing I want to be reminded of.

'I wonder what happened.'

'What if it breaks down,' says Roscoe, 'just when we're upside down hanging over the café.'

'Do you think we'd fall out?' asks Bernie.

'Course we would,' Marie explains. 'You only stay in because you're going round at the same time.'

The man opens the gate to the entrance and we all rush forward. I run not because I'm so excited, but because I'm scared of being at the back. I think it might be worse at the back. There are three on our seat. I'm sandwiched in between Abbi and Bernadette. I feel quite safe with Bernadette. There's so much of her that it's like sitting next to a cushion. Marie is at the front with Roscoe, Jez and Tony. Most of the others from our school are sitting behind them in the front carriage.

We fasten the safety harnesses and wait for the train to fill up. It takes quite a long time. The cable car track is over on our right and we can see people just setting off, reaching the top of the cable and starting to glide downwards. All of a sudden, we see Sister Frances; she's floating past us over-head, riding on a cable car. 'Look out!' shrieks Roscoe at the front of the train. 'The flying nun!'

Everybody falls about. 'Batwomaaaaaan!' sings Jez. Everyone laughs and points.

It looks really funny because it's like a different angle on Sister Frances. Perhaps, *angle* isn't the word to use because, obviously, we're looking at her from underneath, watching her feet waving in the air sticking out underneath her habit and she looks a bit ridiculous. But what surprises me is that Sister looks quite excited. She's holding on tightly to the edge of the car but she's gazing round at everything as if she's really enjoying herself.

It hadn't occurred to me that Sister would go on any rides. 'She seems to be having a good time,' I say to Bernadette.

Bernie looks up. 'Mmmmm,' she says. 'It must be sad to have to go everywhere on your own, though.'

I'd never thought of that. 'Don't you think nuns have friends?' I ask her.

She thinks for a minute. 'Well, they're God's friends, aren't they?'

I suppose they are. But it must still be sad not to have anybody to ride on a cable car with.

We're off. My head gets knocked backwards with the shock as the Corkscrew jerks forward. I feel terrified. I cling on to Bernie at one side of me and Abbi at the other, as the chainlift engages and the train crawls slowly up the first hill. I never find out what the view's like from the top because I've got my eyes closed. I've got my eyes closed and my mouth wide open. Screaming. I keep my eyes closed most of the time. All I'm interested in is hanging on – I cling on to the bar and to Bernie and Abbi – as we're thrown backwards, forwards, side-to-side and my stomach goes up, down and then hovers somewhere in between. The air rushes on to my face; I open my eyes for a second but all I can see is a blur. I don't know where we are. Bernie's saying something but I can't tell what because of the tremendous roar of wind, mixed in with the thundering of our wheels upon the track.

Suddenly, the noise has changed. Someone's switched the lights out. I open my eyes and realize that everything is black. I cling hold of Bernie and scream. 'We're under the lake!' shouts Bernie.

We hurtle forward into the darkness, snaking from side to side. Strange ghostly shapes appear by the side of the walls and cobwebs hang down, brushing on my face. I scream again. On our left we see another Corkscrew hurtling towards us. 'We're going to crash!' yells Abbi. We see the frightened faces of the passengers as they charge down the slope towards us. At the very last second, we make a detour and I see myself sitting in the other train. I let out a sigh of relief. 'It was only a mirror,' I gasp.

The train starts to lose momentum; it rises and falls but much more gently; that gives us chance to keep our eyes open and look at the monsters painted on the walls. Most of the wall is covered in a horrible green slime and there are animals, like rats, scurrying along. I suppose they must be mechanical, like the flying bats round the castle. We turn sharply round a corner to the right and there, just at my eye level, is a rat sitting up on a ledge. It's sitting on its hind legs with its mouth open, snarling, and its sharp yellow teeth are bared as if it's about to spring. I shudder. I think about the children stuck down here when their train broke down – if that were to happen to us, nothing would persuade me to get out of the train and walk.

Another thing we pass that's very clever is a hologram – at least I think it's a hologram. At the side of the track is another mirror. The lighting's a kind of pale crimson and very very dim, so it takes me a while to work out that the moving shape that I can see is really our train winding its way alongside us. It takes even longer to recognize the three of us, huddled up together. Our seat is made for four – although, there's only three of us on it – me, Abbi and Bernadette. In the mirror, though there's someone in the empty place – a strange figure like a ghost. I just have time to focus on the shrouded figure and check again the empty place next to Abbi but, when I look back, the other train has gone, I feel myself coming out in goose pimples. 'Did you see that?' I ask Abbi. But, just then I feel the chain lift engage to pull us out again from underneath the lake.

'Oh no! I bet this'll mean another big drop,' squeals Abbi, clinging hold tightly to my arm.

I'm determined to keep my eyes open, to see what it's like when we come out of the lake. We can see the exit in the distance and the tunnel gets gradually lighter.

Just before we come out, I see something else really weird, I can't make out anything properly because we're still riding along in semi-darkness and the shape is very indistinct. In fact, I think at first I might be seeing things. But, over on my side, we pass a kind of cubby hole in the wall. As we pass, I see a figure peering out. It doesn't look like a ghost. It looks like an old lady. And it looks like the old lady that tried to push Marie into the lake. I grab hold of Bernie and I turn to try to look back and point but it's too late. We've gone too quickly. There's nothing behind but darkness.

The Corkscrew reaches the top of the next slope. There's a sudden flood of light then, before we dare to look down at the view, we crash downwards in a vertical drop somewhere over the *Enchanted Forest*. I close my eyes again, scream, and then cling on to Bernadette and Abbi. I feel petrified. As the train lifts out of the drop, we're once again thrown from side to side – one second I'm dangling upside down, clinging on to the bar for dear life, then I'm turning round, twisting and diving, still leaving my stomach half a kilometre behind.

I can't believe it when the train slows down and we see the queues of people eagerly waiting their turn to be allowed in through the entrance. They must be mad.

The train stops before I feel ready to get out. My head's still spinning and I can't remember where my legs are or how I used to walk on them. I sit back and take a deep breath. 'Come on,' says Bernie, 'we've got to get out.'

A man walks past and unfastens our safety harness and we stagger to our feet. My legs are nearly collapsing. Marie rushes up besides me, her eyes shining with excitement. 'Wasn't it great?' she asks me.

And I can't think what to say.

I go around with Marie for the rest of the day. We get split up from the others because it's a bit too crowded for us all to stay together. At tea-time we go into the Batbar for Batburgers and French Fries washed down with milk shakes and ice-cream. Marie pays for all of it because it really comes to more than I can afford. I don't like Marie paying for me but sometimes she insists. 'Well, I don't want to sit in the café on my own, do I?' she says. 'And I can't sit stuffing myself while you just have a glass of water.'

We've been on lots of rides and we've been to the lake a couple of times to look at the queues for the *Gingerbread House* but each time, they've been massive. We've decided to go back later. I'm not bothered because there's something about the lake that's really scary. I don't mind if we never go on at all. I think it's because of the old woman who tried to push Marie into the water. I can't stop thinking about her. I tell Marie about how I thought I saw her on the *Satan's Staircase*.

'I don't see how you could,' she says, frowning. 'We went past everything so fast.'

'It was that last part – where we slowed down to come out of the lake.'

Marie still looks doubtful. 'It was dark, though, wasn't it?'

I nod. 'It just seemed like her.' I explain.

Marie slurps the remains of her milk shake through her straw. 'Hey,' she says, 'how about Sister Frances, then?'

I start to giggle when I remember how we'd walked past this roundabout called the *Batbreaker*. It wasn't scary – it

107

was for little children really. There was a large figure of a vampire crouched down and there were these – like little aeroplanes, each one shaped like a bat, sort of pivoted on his back. The little bats just went round and round. Marie and I hadn't intended to go on it – we were just walking past when we looked up and saw the familiar long black habit and anorak floating past.

'Oh no,' Marie had cried. 'I just can't believe it.'

Again, Sister looked really excited. She looked as thrilled as the little kiddies who were riding the *Batbreaker* with her. She was hanging on very tightly to the steering wheel between her bat's ears and I even noticed her turning it round and round. Though I'm sure it was just for the children to play with; I don't think it actually steered the bat.

'We ought to buy her a souvenir,' Marie chuckles now. *I rode the Batbreaker and Survived.*

'Aren't we going in the gift shop anyway?'

The gift shop is joined on to the café. There are lots of stalls selling different souvenirs but the shop seems to have the best selection. I haven't brought much money but I do want to buy something for Paul and Carmel and for my mum; I don't know about baby Lianne.

Marie buys lots of silly things – a rubber spider on some elastic and some rubber monsters with magnets on the back that you can fix to fridges and things. She also buys posters showing the view from the top of the *Corkscrew*. She gets some special film to take some photos indoors before we leave. But the thing she likes best of all, is a model of the *Gingerbread House*. It's a money box. It has a slit in the roof to post coins in and a key to open it underneath. She walks away from the check-out carrying her plastic carrier with *Nightmare Park – Journey into Fear* on it.

'Hurry up,' she tells me. 'We want to go back to the lake now.'

Marie doesn't realize how hard it is to buy presents when

you haven't got much money. I want to buy Paul and Carmel something that costs about the same so they won't think one present is better than the other and I want to buy something nice for my mum because she saved up to let me come on the trip. In the end I buy her a little mirror that says, *To the Best Mum in the World*; I buy Paul some playing cards with different monsters on and I get a cardboard cut-out model of *Dracula's Castle* for Carmel to cut out and stick together. I buy baby Liane a stick of Dracula rock. I think it'll be all right for her.

Marie's getting really impatient. 'Have you seen the time?' she says. 'Come on. We're due back at the bus in twenty minutes.'

I pay for my presents and the shop assistant gives me them in a carrier that says *I Rode the Nightmare and Survived*.

Come on. Hurry up,' says Marie, dragging me away.

The lake is very quiet with an eerie mist hovering just above the surface. There are no queues for the boats now. In fact, there are no customers at all. I hadn't realized that it was getting so late; it must be nearly time for the park to close.

One of the ghosts has started roping the gondolas together; he looks up as we both come rushing over. 'We're not too late, are we? Marie asks, switching on her winning, little-girl smile.

I wish we were. I have a feeling of dread. Something I can't understand. It's as if there's something uncanny – something really evil or supernatural – about the lake. I want to tug Marie by the sleeve and hold her back but I don't want her to think I'm a coward. I know how much she's been looking forward to the *Gingerbread House* and I can't let her go in all by herself.

The ghost says nothing. He shakes his head, nudges one

of the gondolas out and brings it over to the jetty. Marie and I hold hands as we step down into the boat. We sit together on the wooden seat as the ghost pushes the boat away from the jetty and we set off towards the island.

The water is very calm. I was expecting to see vibrations from the *Satan's Staircase* but everything is quiet; maybe the Corkscrew's finished for the day.

Suddenly, Marie grabs on to me. 'Keep your head down!'

'What's the matter?'

'Don't turn round.'

I put my head down with Marie, glancing from side to side.

'What is it?'

'It's the dreaded bat.'

'Mmm?'

'The flying nun.'

I giggle. She's talking about Sister Frances. 'Where is she?'

'Just walking past.' Marie clings on to me. 'Don't look.'

'Do you think she's seen us?'

'I don't know. I don't think so.' She glances over her shoulder. 'I think she's going back to the bus.' Marie glances at her watch. 'We're supposed to be there in ten minutes.'

'It won't matter if we're a bit late, will it?'

Marie shakes her head. 'I hope not.'

As we approach the island, we can see the *Gingerbread House* in detail. It has a black cat, like a witch's cat, sitting on the roof asleep. The roof is thatched, but thatched with what look like strands of barley sugar, plaited together. The walls of the house seem to be made of ginger sponge cake and the window frames are like icing, white sugar icing, studded with sweets. I feel as though I could just reach out and break a piece off and eat it.

110

'Now I know what Hansel and Gretel felt like,' Marie marvels, taking out her camera.

I hold Marie's bag and camera case whilst she takes a picture. Suddenly, at one of the cottage windows, I see a figure looking out. It's a witch. She wasn't there before. 'Can you see the witch?' I ask Marie.

'Where?'

I look again and she's gone.

I get the feeling of dread in the depths of my stomach again but I tell myself not to be stupid. I think about the strange figures appearing round *Dracula's Castle*. The witch is probably a hologram.

The ghost pulls up the gondola at the side of the jetty on the island and we stand up and climb out. The island seems to be deserted; I can't see anyone about. We stand and look around. In front of the house there's a sort of little moat, like the one they have around the castle; the water is swishing round and there's a boat hooked up, waiting for us.

The ghost walks to the other side of the gondola and pushes himself away from the jetty; he starts to float back across the lake.

'I've just thought of something,' says Marie.

'What's that?'

'What happens when we come out? I mean, how do we get back to the other side?'

I hadn't thought about that. 'I don't know,' I say.

'Shall we get into the boat?' Marie asks.

'Shouldn't we wait for somebody to come?' I look around again but there's no one about. It seems strangely quiet. Like the silence before a thunderstorm. Surrounding the *Gingerbread House*, there are bushes and trees but they're not even moving; everything is still.

Marie looks round. 'Well, there's nobody here,' she says. 'And we haven't got time to wait, have we?'

I suppose she's right. We walk along the jetty and climb into the boat. Marie reaches over and unties the rope and we set off.

At first, the ride seems very pleasant. The boat travels fairly slowly. We can't control it; it just floats along because the water is moving in the moat.

We don't go straight inside the house. First of all, we come to some black rubbery swing doors that are like a smaller version of the doors they have in hospitals for the stretchers to go through; on the other side of the doors is an area that's like an indoor forest. I try to relax; maybe the ride is going to be all right after all. There are trees and bushes and birds singing and there are wild animals like rabbits and a deer. It's very strange because there's nothing really frightening about things like rabbits and fawns and a badger and yet they all look . . . not scary, but ominous. I suppose all I can say about them is that they just look dead; they look as though they've died and then been stuffed. That's what I don't like about them.

Then it starts to get darker. It's as if the sun is setting really quickly and the moon comes out. Then it is spooky.

There's an owl hooting somewhere and there are uncanny cries that sound like a fox or a wolf. Strange long shadows flitter amongst the trees and there are longer and more eerie howls. I start feeling cold and shivery.

After the forest there's another pair of black rubbery doors but this time they have a portcullis painted on them. When the front of our boat pushes against them, they open and we glide through. It's even darker now.

At first, it's total blackness; we can't see anything at all, but then we start to notice ghostly shapes painted on the walls. Further along there's a dusty, cobweb-covered coffin, lying on the ground. As we approach, the lid starts creaking and it slowly starts to open by itself. Inside is an old, musty grey skeleton. I shudder and rest my hand on Marie's arm. I'm pleased I'm not in here on my own.

Around the next corner is something really obnoxious. It's another coffin that's standing on its side. The coffin is half-open and what we see at first is the inside of the lid that has long, rusty, blood-stained nails sticking out. As we get closer, we can see the body of a woman inside the coffin. It looks as if she's been buried alive. There are blood-covered festering wounds from all the places where the nails are supposed to have stuck inside her body; I'm sure it's only made of plastic, but it turns my stomach over all the same.

'Ugh!' I turn away.

'How revolting!' says Marie. 'How can anybody think of things like that? I mean, what an evil mind they must have.'

I've got a horrible feeling that there are even worse things in store.

The boat turns and floats through another pair of doors – this time, they look like wood, but I think they're just rubber ones again, but painted. This is the proper doorway to the *Gingerbread House* itself. The first part is the cellar. It's very dingy with the only light coming in through two barred windows. It looks like a dungeon. It has bare walls and dusty cobwebs wafting from the stone flagged ceiling. There are large, black spiders dangling down and brown, whiskered rats peering from holes in dark corners.

'Do you think it's too dark to take a photograph?' Marie asks.

I can't understand why she should want to photograph a place like this, 'I don't know.'

And then we come to the cages. As soon as I see the cages, I know there'll be something nasty inside them. The cages are like those in Hansel and Gretel where the witch kept the children prisoner. Our boat floats alongside the first one. It seems to be empty, but then I notice what look like the remains of a fire. On the floor is a pile of black ash and charred wood. I start to smell something pungent and unpleasant; I don't know what it is. Then I notice that on the top of the wood is a pile of bones. I shudder. The bones look much smaller than the ones you get from a butcher's shop, but larger than the bones of a chicken or a bird. I don't know what they are.

Marie takes out her camera and starts to try and focus it. 'It's no good,' she complains. 'It's getting lighter but the boat's moving about too much.'

'Be careful you don't drop it in the water,' I tell her. I sometimes think she's too careless with things that cost so much money.

'I'll put it in my sick bag,' she says, taking out the polythene bag that Sister gave each of us. 'I don't think I'll be needing it now.'

I don't feel so sure. There's another cage in front with a skeleton slumping downwards to the floor. On our right is another cage with what I think is Hansel, pushing his finger through the bars. He's a skeleton as well.

'I thought Hansel and Gretel survived,' says Marie. 'They did in the story, didn't they?'

I try to remember. 'They pushed the witch into the oven, didn't they?'

'Wasn't it Gretel who did that?'

'Mmmm. I think so, but what happened to Hansel, then?'

'I don't know. Perhaps he just starved to death then decayed and turned into a skeleton.'

I pull a face. 'It's a horrible story. I mean, it's supposed to be a fairy story – for little children. I don't know how people can read it to them.

'I think it's good,' says Marie. 'I always liked it when I was little.'

'Well, you're weird aren't you?'

Everything starts to get lighter. The boat goes around a small bend and we get a glimpse of the next scene. Looming up in the distance is the witch's kitchen. We can just see an old-fashioned cooker and a fireplace and the figure of a witch sitting stirring her couldron. 'Oh, Sister Frances,' Marie sighs, 'you didn't really have to come down here and stir our cocoa for us!'

I start to chuckle, but just then the lights go out. Everything is black.

*

I wait for something to happen because I assume, at first, that it's part of the ride. Then I realize something else – something that makes me feel uneasy: the motor has stopped – the motor that drives the water round.

Whilst we've been driving round in the boat, we haven't really noticed the whirring of the motor; you only notice things like that when they stop. Of course it means that the boat has stopped as well. I think we must have broken down.

I cling hold of Marie's wrist. 'What's happened?' I whisper.

'I don't know.'

'Perhaps it's broken down.' I say it jokingly but I don't know why I should laugh about it.

'I think it's part of the ride,' Marie says, but she doesn't sound too confident.

115

'Mmmm.' I remember about the people who got stuck in the *Satan's Staircase*. I can't help feeling worried. I think about the prospect of walking back – through the cellars and ghost train, but then I remember that we can't do that. We can't walk back through water.

We sit and wait. The only sound is the lapping of water around the boat. I try to get my eyes accustomed to the dark, but I can't see anything at all; everything is pitch black.

'What time is it?' I ask Marie.

She lifts her wrist towards her face. 'I don't know. I can't see my watch.'

'I bet it's time we were back at the bus.'

She nods. 'Mmmm. Sister'll be getting mad.'

My stomach sinks with fear. I dread being told off by Sister Frances. I start to feel angry with Marie. It's all her fault. She was the one who wanted to come in here.

'We have got a good excuse, though,' says Marie. 'If the ride's broken down.'

I know we mustn't panic. There's nearly always a sensible explanation but I just wish we weren't waiting in the dark. I wish that we could see. I try once again to focus my eyes in the blackness and I think I can see something move. There seems to be something in front of us, something black and heavy. I cling hold tightly to Marie. 'What is it?' she whispers.

I don't say anything. I try to think of a reasonable explanation. Perhaps someone has found out that the ride's gone wrong and they're coming along to rescue us. But why don't they make a noise? Why don't they call out and ask if we're all right? Why aren't they carrying a torch or something. I feel really frightened.

Marie squashes closer to me. 'Can you see anything?' she whispers.

I open my mouth but I can't say anything. The shape

116

seems to be getting closer. It's very black and tall. I can't think what it can be. I don't know whether Marie can see it or not. I don't want to ask her because I don't want to make a noise. I don't want to move. I don't want it to know we're here.

Suddenly, the boat starts nudging forward.

'Oh, we're off,' Marie sighs and sits back with relief.

I start to relax for a moment but then I realize that it isn't right. The boat's not moving properly; it's only inching forward very slowly. The motor still hasn't been switched on. In fact, the water's not moving at all; only the boat. It's just as if someone's pushing – or it feels more like they're pulling – the boat along. I can't see anybody. I can't even see the dark shape anymore. I feel afraid. I still don't want to speak. I just hold Marie's arm tightly. I don't know what we ought to do.

We cling on tightly to each other and I try not to feel so afraid. I think I ought to say a prayer but I can't think of one that's suitable. I think about Sister Frances, waiting for us in the bus; she has a prayer for everything.

We edge around a corner and it starts to get slowly lighter. We can tell now that there isn't anyone in front. There's certainly no one pulling us, but the end of our rope isn't drifting in the water like it was when we set off. It's lying on the edge as if somebody's left it there. And we're coming up to the witch's kitchen.

The first thing we see is the black, pot-bellied, cast-iron stove then, as we float slowly round the corner, there's the cauldron. The witch is sitting on a stool, stirring the cauldron over a small coal fire. The witch doesn't look up, but she speaks. 'Come in, my dears,' she croaks. 'Come in.'

Marie and I are speechless; we don't know what to do. The boat drifts over towards the edge. The most sensible thing is to ask the witch if something's gone wrong with the ride, but it doesn't seem right to talk to someone who's an exhibit.

I'm not too sure anyway whether the witch is real. We've seen so many things today that looked real but have turned out to be holograms that I don't know what to think. I look at her very closely. She peers at me from underneath the brim of her hat and speaks again. 'Don't be afraid, my darlings. Come inside.'

I stare at her in horror. I feel my body melting as if it could slither into the bottom of the boat. I don't say anything, I just sit and stare. Not only is the witch completely real, but she's the same person who tried to push Marie into the lake. I know she is. I just glare open-mouthed at her.

Marie is already clambering out of the boat. 'Well, that's very kind of you,' she says. I reach to pull her back but she's already standing on the edge.

'We wondered if the ride had broken down,' Marie explains.

'Come in, my dears. Come in.'

I don't want to follow Marie, but I can't let her go on her own. I start to get up. I remember that Marie never saw the old lady properly. I was the only one who saw her face. Marie doesn't even know there's any danger.

'We should have been back at our bus,' Marie explains. 'Our teachers will be waiting for us.'

The witch stops stirring her cauldron and gives Marie a toothless smile.

I step out of the boat and into the witch's kitchen. It's actually quite small. There's the stove and the fire and the cauldron and a three-legged stool and behind them is a backcloth like scenery on a stage. It has old-fashioned cupboards and a kind of dresser painted on it. Fastened on to the backcloth are what seem to be some real shelves; I walk across and have a look.

Ranged along the shelves is a strange assortment of glass jars, bottles, decanters, tiny enamel tins and cardboard boxes. Some of the jars have obnoxious-looking contents – the kind of things you find in a biology lab at school – things that once were warm and alive and are now peeled naked and preserved.

Along the shelf, underneath the containers, is a row of labels each one hand-drawn in Gothic script.

'We wondered if you might be able to help us,' Marie says to the witch.

I read *Newt's Liver* and *Rat's Blood*, *Hedgehog Entrails* and *Ground Tadpoles*.

The witch holds up her ladle which is filled with a blood-coloured thick greasy liquid. 'Would you like a drink, dear?' she asks Marie.

'Well, it's very kind of you,' says Marie, 'but no thanks. Er, we've just had our tea.'

Ravens' Eyeballs, I read. *Piglets' Toenails* and *Dried Frogsblood*. I start feeling slightly sick.

'We wondered if you could help us get out,' Marie explains. 'We ought to be back at the car park by now.'

The witch nods her head as if she's deep in thought. 'Mmmm,' she mutters. 'Mmmm.'

Her cauldron is heated over a coal fire; as I get nearer I can see that inside the coals is a red electric light bulb with one of those flicker-things on top that you have in electric fires. I feel very confused; I don't know what's real and what isn't.

Fastened on the wall is a shrunken head. It's very small and wizened with long straight black hair. The skin looks tight and wrinkled and the eyes are dry and staring.

The witch stands up and takes off her pointed hat. Her hair is long and black and greasy but I think it must be a wig. Her hair was grey when she tried to push Marie into the lake.

The witch walks across to the shrunken head and then she reaches out and touches it. I shudder. In fact, she doesn't just touch it; she turns it; it's actually the handle of a cupboard. The witch opens the door and hangs her hat inside. Underneath her long black cloak, she's wearing a pair of black boots but they don't look very old-fashioned; they just look like over-the-ankle boxer boots. I see a flash of something green around her legs. I think she's wearing a track suit underneath her cloak.

The witch closes the cupboard door then twists the head of a small bat hanging on the wall. It's another doorway; she reaches inside and switches on a light. There seems to be another room.

'Is there a telephone anywhere?' Marie asks her.

The witch says nothing but walks inside the back room. She leaves the door open, so we peer inside. It's very strange – well, what I mean is that it isn't strange at all – it's very modern and it looks like somebody's flat. It has kitchen units and an automatic washer and a microwave. I just can't understand it.

The witch walks up to another, ordinary, door. She opens it then turns and faces us. She pauses. 'I'll see what I can do for you, my dears,' she says. This time she says it in a normal voice. She seems to have forgotten to croak. Or maybe she only croaks when she's sitting in her kitchen. I don't know. She stares very hard at Marie. 'Yes,' she says, 'you wait here for a short while and I'll see what I can do.'

She gives a little cackle as she walks out of the door and leaves us on our own.

We both stare at each other for a second then start looking round the flat. 'I think she must live here,' says Marie.

It certainly looks like it. Somebody lives here, anyway.

Next to the kitchen is a kind of study. There are some bookshelves and a desk with a word processor on it. 'I wonder what she uses that for,' I say in amazement.

Marie shakes her head. 'I don't know.'

I've never seen anything like it – a flat inside a spooky ride! What a weird place to live.

Marie has a nosy round the kitchen but I'm fascinated by the word processor; I can't imagine what she could use it for.

Next to it on the desk is a folder. There's a label on the cover with the same hand-written Gothic script that I've seen on the jars in the kitchen – the outside kitchen. It says: *Journey into Nightmare – the Story of a Witch*.

"Did you recognize her?" I ask Marie.

'What do you mean?'

I peep inside the cover of the folder. 'She's the woman who tried to push you into the lake.'

Marie turns round and stares at me. 'She can't be,' she says incredulously. 'Are you sure?'

I nod my head. 'Positive.'

Inside the folder is a letter from a publisher:

SIRENBOOKS

374 Pompadour Lane, London WC1E 3AL

Dear Ms Ranmoor

Thank you very much for sending us *Journey into Nightmare –
the true story of a Witch* which we have read with great interest.

Although your story certainly makes for compulsive reading,
we really feel that the plot is much too unlikely to be given
serious consideration by the modern reader of today and so
we are regretfully returning the manuscript to you.

We hope you will soon be able to place it elsewhere.

With best wishes

Samantha Stocksbridge.

Samantha Stocksbridge
Fiction Editor

'Well, I hope she gets us out soon,' Marie says. 'Sister Frances'll be going bananas.'

I'm still fascinated by the folder. I'd like to see the manuscript that the publishers have turned down but I don't want the witch to come back and find me snooping. I leave the file and look around the room.

On the opposite wall is a framed picture of a class of schoolchildren. They look a bit old-fashioned; they're standing in rows in their uniforms, posing, and their teacher is seated at the front. She looks like the witch; I think it could be her daughter or a younger sister. I look more closely and notice that some of the pupils in the photo have little crosses over their heads. I wonder what it means — maybe they were the prefects. I don't know. There's a cross above a boy with a big square head and another smaller podgy boy; another one over a tall slim boy and a dark-haired girl and another girl who looks the spitting image of Marie. 'Look at this,' I tell her. 'There's a girl here that looks just like you.'

Marie is not impressed. 'Ugh' she says, when she sees the photo. 'She looks really old-fashioned. You don't think I look like that, do you? Look at her shoes!'

'I don't mean her clothes, I mean, just what she looks like.'

'Well, I don't think so,' Marie scoffs.

I think about the folder again. The witch hasn't come back yet; maybe I could just have another peep at it. I walk across to the door and peer outside. There doesn't seem to be anybody about. There's just a dark passageway and some steps. I close the door and walk back over to the desk. Then I open the file at the next page and start to read.

JOURNEY INTO NIGHTMARE
THE STORY OF A WITCH

Synopsis

This is the true story of Agnes, a schoolteacher who became a witch. And this is how it began.

Agnes was a schoolmistress. She taught Latin and Classical Studies at Salmon Pastures Girls' Grammar School, a school with a fine reputation for hard work and discipline which was set in an exclusive part of town.

Agnes had obtained a first class honours degree in classics; she was an efficient and hard-working teacher but she seemed to find it difficult to hold her pupils' interest. At first they would talk amongst themselves in class; then they called her names in low voices when she came past, then they began the practical jokes — girls made rude noises in the classroom and Agnes found unmentionable articles scattered around her desk on more than one morning. Then the girls became downright disobedient: some classes would burst into laughter whenever Agnes tried to reprimand them; some would make so much noise that it was impossible to hear herself speak; others would refuse point blank to do anything Agnes asked them.

Fortunately, the headmistress of the grammar school was an excellent disciplinarian. Whenever Agnes reached the end of her tether, when she thought she could tolerate the girls' behaviour no longer, all she had to do was threaten to send for Miss Rowlinson, and the girls would become like angels.

All went well until the school was re-organized and became Salmon Pastures Comprehensive. This school had no place for a teacher of Latin. As Agnes had no other subject to offer, she was given classes of restless low ability boys and girls and asked to teach them Social Studies or Personal Education and Life Skills – subjects in which her pupils had little interest and which failed to carry the incentive of examination success. Miss Rowlinson swiftly took early retirement and the new young headmaster was more concerned with proving popular with his pupils than helping a middle-aged woman with problems of classroom control.

Agnes would have considered retirement herself if her mother had not been ill, but she needed her wages to pay her mother's private hospital fees. Agnes loved her mother. She had lived with her for fifty years, never marrying and seldom making any friends. Nothing but the best private clinic was good enough and she felt that she would die rather than give up her job and let her mother end her days in poverty.

The new comprehensive school pupils soon learned to exploit Agnes's weakness. Lessons became a battleground with Agnes always the loser. The pupils learned nothing in class apart from how to wear down their teacher and their parents soon began to complain about children being injured in fights in the classroom their property being thrown out of windows and a teacher who was incapable of exerting any control.

Worry and stress began to take their toll on Agnes. Her nerves became so bad that she could seldom sleep at night. In the classroom she would stare for long periods at the wall, apparently in a trance, then make strange jerking movements. She lost interest in her appearance: her hair was greasy and unkempt, her clothes were shabby and old-fashioned. Agnes was not only losing control of her pupils but losing her self-respect as well.

It was 4R who finally destroyed Agnes the teacher and set her on the path to becoming Agnes the witch. Their ringleader was a young man called Roger, a cretinous youth, built like a haystack with a head that seemed almost completely rectangular. When Agnes asked him to sit down in his place, he swore at her; he *molested girls in the stockroom on the pretext of sharpening his pencil and the only time he ever picked up a pen was to inscribe the name of the local football team on any surface he could find.*

Roger seemed to delight in making Agnes's life a misery. Whenever anything unfortunate happened, Roger was always around. When she lost her footing on the school staircase, Roger happened to be walking behind her; when a pair of football boots landed on her head, Roger was looking out of the window at the time and when she was locked inside the classroom all night, Roger was the last pupil seen in school.

It was two days after this last event that Agnes went to pieces. Standing on the school stage with the rest of the staff, singing All things Bright and Beautiful, *Agnes caught sight of Roger's face at the back of the hall and felt herself bursting into tears. In order to cover up her distress, she then started laughing instead. Even the loudest singing of the staff could not drown out Agnes's hysterical laughter. The head, who had been looking for an excuse to get rid of Agnes anyway, insisted that she would have to leave the school.*

Agnes should have felt relieved but she was already in the throes of a nervous breakdown when she was forced to take her mother away from her private nursing home and try to care for her at home. Shortly afterwards, her mother died and Agnes could never forgive herself. She blamed herself and most particularly the pupils in 4R for the death of the only person she had ever been close to.

During the next two years, Agnes felt distressed at anything which reminded her of these events. She felt nauseous at seeing a bus heading for Salmon Pastures and catching sight of a jar of salmon fishpaste in the local supermarket nearly made her faint. She thought the best thing would be to move. Her mother had been well-insured and Agnes had a tidy sum to invest. A boarding house at Blackpool she thought would be the answer.

Agnes planned a week-end break in Blackpool and spent many hours talking to estate agents and wandering round the streets looking at faded, neglected boarding houses and small hotels. There wasn't one in which she thought she could feel happy.

She went for a walk along the promenade and, desperate for a cup of tea, called in the Magnolia Café. It was here that Agnes became acquainted with Mr Brad Field, a gentleman who owned the Blackpool Ghost Train and who was wanting to sell up because ill health and a broken marriage were forcing him to move.

Agnes bought the ghost train. She enjoyed the work at first as it involved little more than sitting in a ticket booth, taking money and adding it up at the end of the day. What did upset Agnes, though, were the teenagers. Some of them were rowdy, rude and high-spirited and they resurrected all of Agnes's worst fears. She started to have terrible nightmares about the teenagers who came on her ghost train. She became obsessed with thoughts of violence and murder. She read books about the lives of notorious killers and spent many hours staring at exhibits in the Chamber of Horrors in the nearby wax museum.

Agnes might have carried on like this, a harmless eccentric, were it not for the fact that one day a young man entered the ghost train who seemed a replica of the fearful Roger. He was a similar height and weight, he had the same peculiar-shaped head and a similar level of intelligence. When he decided to climb out of the ghost train to mess about and scare his friends, Agnes's control snapped. The young man was never seen again.

It was a few months later that Agnes heard about the new theme park that was offering spaces to people who wanted to hire or buy a ride. Agnes was enthusiastic. She decided to leave Blackpool and set up at the new theme park. It sounded ideal. The surroundings also gave her opportunities to observe teenagers coming to the park. She took out a photograph of 4R and hung it on her wall. Roger already had a cross marked over his head. It would not be long before the rest of 4R were to meet with a similar fate.

I start to feel worried. I put the file down on the desk and walk back to the photograph on the wall. I look at it more carefully. I look at the big boy with the square head with the cross marked over him. I look at the teacher. I look at her very closely. I can see now why I thought it must be her daughter or her sister: it was taken, about ten years ago and she looked a lot younger then. But I'm sure it's her. It's Agnes.

I turn round to Marie, but she's busy taking photographs. I try to think things out. If Agnes . . . the witch . . . if the witch is Agnes then . . . the thought is horrific, like pushing my fingers inside an electric socket in my head, but I try to stay calm and think it through. If Agnes is the witch and if this really is a true story, then that could explain why the teenagers have gone missing at *Nightmare Park*. It could also explain why she tried to push Marie into the lake. I look at the picture again, at the blonde-haired girl with the cross marked over her head. I look back at Marie. Even though she has a camera up to her face, I can still see the resemblance. It all starts making sense.

'I think we're in danger, Marie.'

It could also explain why the ride stopped here – just outside the witch's kitchen. I start feeling very frightened.

Marie isn't taking any notice. 'It's a good job I got this 1000 ASA film,' she says. 'I couldn't have taken any in here without it.'

'Marie.' I speak to her more urgently.

'What's the matter?'

'We've got to get away. I don't think there's time to explain all the reasons now.'

129

We can't go in the boat and there isn't another door. But we've got to go before the witch comes back.

'What's up?'

'I think she wants to kill you.'

'You what?'

We have to get away. Or if we can't get away, then we have to find somewhere to hide. I start to look round the room. Just then I hear footsteps coming up the steps. 'I think she's after us,' I say to Marie. 'We've got to get away.'

Marie doesn't seem to understand. I start to panic. I feel very very frightened. Something's going to happen; I know it is.

The footsteps are coming nearer. She's reached the top of the steps. I look desperately round the room. We can't go in the oven; we can't hide under the desk; the cauldron's full of blood soup. Then I remember the cupboard – the cupboard where she hung her hat. 'Come on. In here.' I grab Marie and pull her inside the door.

'This is stupid,' she says to me. 'She's not a proper witch, you know.'

There isn't enough room for both of us because of a bagful of clothing on the floor. I pick it up and hold it, then shuffle to the back. I'm just about to pull the door closed when Agnes pounces into the room. I leave the door so she doesn't hear a noise. I peer out through the slit.

'Right, my dears!' we hear her cackling. 'I'm coming to get you now.'

I hear her footsteps walking past and I try to hold myself still. I swallow hard. I have to try and keep calm. Then I see her standing in front of the crack. At first I can't see what she looks like because the crack's too narrow; I just notice the patch of black. As she moves away from the door, though, and I get a proper view of her, I nearly faint with horror. She's leering like a maniac and wielding a sharpened broomstick.

I feel terrified. I hold myself rigid. I want to scream but I stop myself. I mustn't move and I mustn't make any sound. We just have to stand, completely motionless. I want to faint but I have to keep upright. I mustn't let my legs sink. My hand is wrapped round Marie's wrist. I grip it tightly, like a vice. We both stand completely rigid. We hold tightly on to each other and stop breathing.

We hear the witch running round the room. 'Come on now!' she croaks. 'Where are you?'

I try to concentrate on the cupboard – on the bag. I have to focus my attention to stop myself from screaming. A ray of light is shining in the cupboard and it's lighting up the top of my black plastic bag. There's a blue demin jacket on the top and the edge of a football scarf. They seem rather strange clothes for a woman like Agnes to wear but, there again, I tell myself, Agnes is a very strange person.

I hear a banging noise; it sounds as if Agnes is hitting things with the broomstick. 'I'm coming to find you now, my dears,' Agnes croaks. There's another banging noise and a swish. I think she's poking the broomstick into the water. 'I know you're round here somewhere.'

I set my jaws together to stop them from chattering. I mustn't make any noise. I want to see what's happening but I daren't look. Then I hear a clambering and a splash. It sounds as if Agnes is putting something into the boat. Or . . . my heart lifts up . . . maybe she's climbing into the boat herself. Maybe she thinks we've run away and she's setting off to look for us. I still can't see anything but I strain my ears to interpret every sound. I think she's got some oars. I think she might be rowing away.

I can hardly believe it. I daren't relax and I feel terrified of opening the cupboard door, but I know we've got to get away. If Agnes has gone then this is our only chance. We mustn't come out too soon, but we mustn't wait too long. We must escape.

I tentatively push the cupboard door. I peer around the corner. The kitchen seems to be empty. I put down my bag and creep to the water's edge. The boat has gone and the water is slapping against the wall. The witch has just rowed round the corner. I let out my breath in a huge long sigh. 'Come on.' I wait for Marie to come out of the cupboard.

In the end I have to drag her out. I can't understand what's happened to her. She's hopeless. She just stands there like a cornered rabbit. She isn't usually like that. 'What about the door?' she says at last. 'The door the witch went out of.'

We run straight towards it.

'Where do you think it leads?' Marie whispers.

I don't have to think for long. 'To *Satan's Staircase*,' I tell her. 'To the tunnel under the lake.' That must be why I saw Agnes down there.

We run out through the door and along a narrow passageway. Then we come to a spiral iron staircase. There are handles at the side. Marie goes down first and I follow; we stay close together all the time.

At first, my legs are like jelly and I can hardly climb down the stairs but I know we have to get away. If we sit down and wait until we feel OK, it'll be much too late. I force myself to hurry up.

I want to tell Marie about the book, but I need to save my breath. I think as well about the Corkscrew that stopped with the teenagers on. Everything's falling into place. I want to tell Marie but we're running much too fast.

The stairs go down a long long way. I think about the tunnel underneath the lake and how I felt I could never walk through it on my own. But I don't feel scared of things like that now. None of the ghosts and things are real – they're only made-up. Agnes is real and she really wants to kill us.

At last, the bottom is in sight. There's some kind of dim

emergency lighting just like tiny torches but at least it means we can see our way around.

We sprint down the last few metres and stand, gasping, in another narrow passageway. There's an opening in front that looks like the actual tunnel that the Corkscrew runs through. We just wait a couple of seconds to get our breath.

'Do you think there's another way down?' Marie asks. She's looking towards the end of the passage and I know what she's thinking. We mustn't assume we're safe. Agnes could have come down here a different way. We'll have to be very careful.

'I don't know.' I tell her. 'We'd better have a look.' Marie goes off in front.

We tiptoe along the narrow passageway. My legs are so weak that I hold my hands on the walls to stop myself from collapsing. The walls are made of stone and they feel very cold. When we get to the end, we pull back into the shadows. No one can see us here.

Marie peers round the corner to the left.

'Is it safe?' I ask her.

'I think we're all right that way.'

Suddenly, I hear a noise. A clanging noise with an echo. It sounds like a door opening. Marie turns her head and looks round to the right. 'Oh no.'

'What is it?' I can't bear her to tell me.

Marie closes her eyes as if she's about to faint. 'It's her. She's coming down the tunnel.'

I feel as if my strength has gone, as if I can't find the energy to walk up the steps again.

'She didn't see you?' I hardly dare ask Marie. 'Did she?'

'No. She was just coming round the corner.'

I pause for a moment and take a breath. 'We'll have to go back up.'

Marie nods.

There must be another way down, another staircase. I feel exhausted, but the thought does occur to me that we're both younger than Agnes; we're both healthy; we can run upstairs faster than she can. 'Come on.'

We start off back again.

I just concentrate on the stairs, nothing else. Pushing my feet down; turning the corner; panting. We're going to get there, I tell myself. We're going to get away. We're going to escape.

I'm afraid to reach the top in case Agnes is there already with her broomstick waiting to pounce but I tell myself she can't be. She can't run up stairs as fast as we can. I try to think of all the other things on our side: there are two of us and we're both fairly clever. We might be able to trick her. We could push her into the water. I think of Gretel and how she tricked the witch and pushed her into the oven. I suddenly feel determined to survive. 'Come on,' I tell Marie. 'Let's hurry up.'

'Hang on.' Marie's dragging behind. I start feeling impatient with her. Marie's normally the one who takes control. I wish she'd hurry up.

I wait for her. As I pause for a second, I start thinking of ways to escape. We could swim back. We could take off our clothes and dive into the water. We could balance on the rail at the edge of the water, or if Agnes is after us, we could find the other staircase – the way that she came down.

I reach down my hand and help to pull Marie. 'Come on,' I tell her. 'We're nearly there now.'

We reach the top and pause as we try to get our breath back. We stand and face each other. 'We've got to escape,' I tell Marie.

She stands gasping. She doesn't say anything at all.

'We'll take the evidence with us – your camera – the photo on the wall. We can even take the book.'

I suddenly think of the black plastic bag I was holding,

with the jacket and the football scarf inside. I shudder. Blue denim jackets were what the boy and girl were wearing when they disappeared beside the lake.

'We'll take the scarf and the jacket as well.'

Marie doesn't even know what I'm talking about. She just stands there pale and frightened. I feel terrified but I also feel determined that we're going to get away. I think about when my dad lived at home and how he used to be when he came back drunk in the afternoon. I used to hide Paul and Carmel upstairs. Before I did that, though, I used to move things out of the way – anything that he could hurt us with. I don't think Marie has ever been in any danger like that. She doesn't seem to know what to do.

'Come on.' I hold Marie's hand as we creep down the passageway towards the kitchen. The door's still open. I peer inside. I can't see any sign of Agnes. I listen. There are no footsteps; no sound of oars in the water.

I remember the photo I took of Agnes when she tried to push Marie into the lake. We've got to get the camera back.

I can see where we put our bags down by the desk. 'Come on, let's get the bags,' I tell Marie. 'Pick up your camera. We've got to get all the photos.'

I creep inside and tiptoe over to my bag. I read the slogan: *I Rode the Nightmare and Survived*. I only wish it was true. I just want to go home and give the presents to Paul and Carmel and Liane. I want my mum to smile and hug me when I give her the little mirror. I want to cry.

Marie is still standing at the doorway, pale and wide-eyed. 'Come on,' I tell her. 'Get your bag. We're going to escape.'

I take the photo off the wall and place it inside my bag. Then I take the folder, *The Story of a Witch* and place that beside the picture. Last of all, I go in the cupboard and open the plastic bag. I feel weak and faint as I take out the jacket and the scarf but I take them out anyway and place them on top of my carrier. I look around and try to decide what to do.

If we swim, we might not be able to get away if Agnes comes after us in the boat. And I can't take the bag with me if I swim. The other thing is to balance along the edge of the water, on the rail. 'Come on,' I tell Marie. 'We'll walk back along the edge.'

We start off walking sideways very slowly, holding hands. Then we get more confident. There's room for us both to walk along in single file. We set off around the corner that leads towards the dungeons.

It's very dark, but the rail is raised up slightly and we can see it stretching before us. I concentrate all my attention on it, watching out for a break, for any place where we could slip into the water. All the time as well, I'm listening, listening for footsteps or the splashing of a boat. The only sounds are the rustling of our carrier bags, the panting of our breath and the pounding of our heartbeats. Apart from that, it's deathly quiet.

It seems a long way to the dungeons. It didn't seem as far as this when we were in the boat. I start to wonder whether there might be another turn off – something that we've missed, but the rail isn't broken anywhere and the water is there below us. This must be the way that we came. We carry on.

Suddenly, there's a noise. We both stand still and freeze. It's a far-off echoing sound like the closing of a door again. 'What is it?' whispers Marie.

'I don't know.' I listen again. 'It seemed a long way off.' I wait, straining my ears. I can't hear anything else.

We turn the corner and see the outline of the cages ahead. I would never have thought that I could walk through them in the dark, but the cages don't seem frightening anymore. The only thing to be frightened of is Agnes.

After a few metres, we enter the actual dungeon. That

means that we can move off the rail and walk on the floor again. I can see the outline of the cage in front with the skeleton of Hansel glowing in the dark. He's still holding the bone out through the bars. I want to laugh but I know I mustn't get hysterical.

We start to tiptoe towards the cages. I'm still holding Marie by the hand, but when she turns the corner and sees Hansel in his cage, she pulls me back. She looks terrified. 'Come on.' I try to lead her forwards.

Marie just stands there shaking her head. It's as if she's dissolving in terror. 'Come on.' I try to urge her gently.

She just stands frozen to the spot.

I keep listening, straining my ears for any kind of sound. I'm not sure whether I can hear anything or not. 'Come on, Marie.'

Still she doesn't move.

I listen again. I think there might be the sound of a boat rowing through the water, but I'm not sure. It could just be my imagination.

I look out for somewhere to hide. At the other end of the dungeons, there's a dark corner just where the boat first comes through the swing doors. I think we ought to head towards it.

'Come on.'

I start to feel cross with Marie. She's the one who normally gives the orders and now she seems incapable of anything at all. I feel like shouting at her but we've got to keep quiet and I mustn't make her more upset. I think about the way I talk to the twins when they start being awkward. 'We're going over there, look.' I point to the dark corner of the dungeon. 'We're going to hide.' I try to sound reassuring. 'We're going to get away then.' I make my voice sound as confident as I can. 'We're going to escape.'

I nod my head at Marie as if I'm talking to a four-year-old. I even give her a smile of encouragement though I don't know where I can get it from. 'Come on.'

I pull her along and she follows me around the cages and over towards the darkened corner. Her body is rigid like a marionette and she doesn't say anything at all.

I think I can hear the splash of water. It sounds like a boat; it seems to be getting nearer. I try not to look at the grotesque shapes in the darkness: whiskered rats, skeletons and black, blood-speckled bats.

We reach the dark corner behind the first cage and crouch down.

I sit with one arm round Marie and the other clapsed tightly round my carrier bag. Although I can't read the slogan, I remember it: *I Rode the Nightmare and Survived.* That's all I want. I want to get out of here alive.

'Somebody's coming.' Marie's voice sounds like a croak. It's as if she can hardly speak.

'She won't be able to see us here.' I say that but straightaway I'm not too sure. When we came past in the boat, we were facing the front. When someone is rowing a boat, then they face behind. She only needs to look up when she goes past. She only needs to look up once to see us.

I feel terrified. I look around, but there's nowhere else to hide. There isn't time anyway. The boat is coming nearer. I can hear the sound of the water slapping against the edge. I can hear the splash and then the pause and then the water dripping from the oars.

I remember Marie's story about the two girls trapped with the monsters. It's as if we're living the story out. It's just as if we're Hanzel and Kimberley hiding in *Dracula's Castle.* And then I remember what Sister Frances said about the ending: about the powers of evil. I wish that Marie had altered the ending, the way that Sister said. I wish she'd written a happy ending where the two girls were rescued. I wish that the forces of evil had been defeated and good had triumphed. The boat's getting really close.

I don't know what to do. I want to scream and cry out but

138

I know that the only chance we've got is to hide here, as quiet as we can. The noise comes again but nearer: the splash and then the drip of water from the oars. I feel faint as I cling on to Marie. I try to remember about Hansel and Gretel. Perhaps we ought to jump out on the witch and push her into the water. But I know I couldn't do that. I couldn't kill anybody. I couldn't do what Gretel did and push the witch inside the lighted oven. I can't do anything at all. And still the boat comes nearer. Splash, Pause. Drip. Splash. Pause. Drip.

I think about saying a prayer, but I can't remember one. I remember a bit from the psalms. *Yea, though I walk . . .* what is it? *Yeah though I walk through the valley of the shadow of death*, I find myself muttering it under my breath. *I will fear no evil*. I think this must be the valley of the shadow of death; it certainly seems like it. But I do fear the evil. I'm terrified out of my skin.

Then I see the boat. I see the edge of it nosing through the tunnel. I nearly collapse and slither through the floor. I see the wooden point of the boat and the black figure seated inside and then the oars and the long arms plunging them into the water. I feel as though I'm nearly dead with shock when I suddenly notice something else: the black hooded figure has a circle of white around its head. It has a silver crucifix gleaming in the dark. I nearly throw myself at her with relief. There, red-faced, puffing and panting, rowing along for all she's worth, with her habit tucked up inside her long black woolly socks, is our saviour, Sister Frances.

We get our first award in school assembly. Somebody comes over from the police department and presents Marie and myself with a certificate and a cheque. That's only the first reward. The police inspector tells us that, later on, we'll be invited to a ceremony at the police headquarters. There'll be another presentation and Marie, myself and Sister Frances will be taken there in a special chauffeur-driven car.

'Let's just pray they won't let Sister near the steering wheel,' Marie mutters under her breath.

The award is supposed to be for bravery but, I must admit, I don't really feel as though we did anything very brave. I think we did the same as anyone else would. I mean, if a maniac is chasing after you with a sharpened broomstick, you don't just sit there. All we did was run away. But we took the photos and everything as well – all the evidence to convict her.

Sister has based her sermons on Nightmare Park ever since. She's told everyone how she felt moved by the Holy Spirit to come and look for us. 'I felt there was something wrong,' she announced to all the school. 'I had seen Teresa and Marie heading towards the island, but then when I prayed, there was no mistaking the message – they were in danger. I had to go and play my part.'

Everybody sniggers at this because, when Marie and I told them about Sister rowing round the corner, red-faced, with her habit tucked into her socks, they thought it was hilarious. Marie even said she was going to organize a poster competition for the best illustration of the event.

Sister has also told us all to pray for Agnes. We're

140

supposed to be praying for her soul. 'Personally,' says Marie, 'I think we ought to pray for Sister to retake her driving test. I think she's twice as dangerous and she's still out driving down the streets!'

Sister has explained to us all that she's now visiting Agnes in prison. 'I've taken her a small present this week,' she explains. 'A book that has been my inspiration – the *Revelation of St Julian*. And a box of Liquorice All Sorts.' She gazes round the hall with her antennae bristling at the smirking faces of the fourth year. 'And I think it would be a good idea if some of you were to send her cards or little presents. I think we all could be supportive to her at what must be a most difficult time.'

'We could send her a cookery book!' Marie whoops in the cloakroom afterwards. '*A Thousand and One Ways to Serve Frogs' Eyeballs*.'

'*Cocktail Snacks with Newts and Lizards Blood*.'

'Can you just imagine them together?' Marie asks. The two most fearful women in the world? The other prisoners must be terrified.

'What?' says Abbi. 'Of having Agnes in the prison?'

'No.' Marie scoffs. 'Of Sister Frances. Just imagine.' She walks around the cloakroom with her hands clasped in front of her, 'Repent! Repent! Have a Liquorice All Sort. Repent! Repent!'

We never get round to watching the video of Nightmare Park; in fact we've donated it to Mr Hoyland. Apparently he's given it to the college for lessons with the students on How Not to Make a Video. As it highlights all the worst mistakes that people can make, they've found it extremely useful.

In spite of the video, Ms Maltby manages to pass her teaching practice. It seems that Mr Hoyland told the college that she'd played a part in helping to catch a psychopathic

141

murderer and they seemed to think that was good enough. In the end, I go and confess about my part in locking Ms Maltby in the stockroom. It was when I thought about Agnes's story that I started to get worried. I don't think Ms Maltby will turn into a psycopathic murderer but, just in case she does, I want my conscience to be clear.

I know that sometimes, when you go through a really bad experience, it can turn your mind funny – like it did with Agnes. I think she'll always be mad. Even though Sister is lighting candles for her, I don't suppose she'll ever really recover. Sometimes though, I think a frightening experience can make you feel good about yourself. That's what seems to have happened with me.

The reason I was able to escape and to look after Marie and collect all the evidence from the witch's kitchen wasn't because I was particularly brave; it was just because I made my mind up. I made my mind up to escape. And once I'd decided that, the rest seemed fairly easy. I think that perhaps you can do most things if you feel really determined about them.

I was a bit surprised as well about Marie. I'd never seen Marie having to cope with anything dangerous before so I just took it for granted that she'd be braver than me. I suppose I assumed that because she's cleverer than me and richer than me and she lives in a really big house. When it came to escaping from Agnes though, and collecting the evidence together, I was better than she was. I don't think any worse of Marie – in fact, sharing it all has brought us closer together. It's just made me realize that being different doesn't mean that one of us is always better than the other.

When I bought the mirror for my mum and the cut-out castle and playing cards and the rock for Liane in the gift shop, I never thought they would mean so much to me. A friend of my mum has made a special display case to put them in together with my certificate and the carrier bag.

They're on show in our front room, over the top of the sideboard. Sometimes when I sit and look at them I remember. I think about sitting in the dungeon in the dark, waiting for Agnes to come rowing through the doors, remembering what was written on my bag and wishing it was true.

Now it is true. When I'm playing with the twins or watching the television, I look up sometimes and grin to myself. Yes, I think: I really did it. I really have got something to be proud of. I would never have thought that the words could ever be so important: *I Rode the Nightmare and Survived.*

STEVIE DAY SUPERSLEUTH
(that's me!)

I'm on my way to being the first female Commissioner of the Metropolitan Police. It's true I have a few personal problems: for a start I'm small and skinny and people are always mistaking me for a boy. I'm 14 – though you wouldn't think so – and my younger sister, Carla, not only looks older than me but she's much prettier too. Not that that really matters. You see, she doesn't have my brains.

If you want to see my razor-sharp mind in action or have proof of my brilliant powers of deduction then read about my triumphant successes in:

STEVIE DAY: Supersleuth
STEVIE DAY: Lonely Hearts
STEVIE DAY: Rat Race

ARMADA